JOHNNIE'S BLITZ

Bombs are raining down on London and Johnnie Stubbs is on the run from the law. His dad is in the army and he has no mother. So Johnnie hides out with his grandad and some other dodgy relatives in a caravan near a rubbish tip.

When a bomb drops nearby a traumatized three year old wanders over to the site. Johnnie decides that he has to find the girl's parents and return her to them, even if this means that the police catch up with him. But London is where Johnnie might find Shirley's parents and bombs or no bombs that is where they go. Are Shirley's family still alive? Will Johnnie manage to elude the police long enough to find out?

An exciting tale that vividly brings wartime Britain to life.

Bernard Ashley

JOHNNIE'S BLITZ

BARN OWL BOOKS

FOR PAUL, CARL, ROSIE AND LUKE

Johnnie's War was first published by Viking in 1995
This edition was first published 2003 by Barn Owl Books,
157 Fortis Green Road, London N10 3LX

ISBN 978-1-9030-1528-5

Designed and typeset by Douglas Martin Associates, Oadby
Printed and bound by CPI Bookmarque, Croydon
Barn Owl Books are distributed by Frances Lincoln
4 Torriano Mews, Torriano Avenue, London NW5 2RZ

ACKNOWLEDGEMENTS

I should like to thank especially Esi Eshun and Jenny Nix for their help with my research for the book. Grateful thanks are also due to Fay Cattini, Cyril Demarne OBE, Eleanor Hage and Jonathan Riddell (of the London Transport Museum).

1

THE GERMANS were hitting hard. It was autumn 1940 and that first sudden Saturday air raid on the East End of London had killed and wounded people and pets, flattened houses and damaged the docks. Now having raiders in the sky looked like becoming a nightly business – a deadly business – and Johnnie Stubbs cursed the war that had turned his life upside down. His dad had been called up to be a soldier – he had no mum – and nights were now spent huddling in an air raid shelter in his grandad's scrap yard on the south side of the river Thames in Plumstead.

The outdoor shelters in people's gardens were supposed to be 'Andersons, those corrugated arches of metal covered in sandbags and about the size of sheds. But Grandad Stubbs hadn't bought one of those – he'd picked up a wide, heavy metal door off a bombed factory site, put bricks and sandbags round three sides and strong mesh across the front. It was stuck out in the scrap yard because they'd never get it into the caravan; and there it sat between the vehicles with a tarpaulin flung over it.

There hadn't been much warning of the raid tonight. The siren had gone and the three of them – Johnnie, Grandad and Old Nell, Grandad's wife – had come scuttling out of the caravan as the drone of the German aircraft became a threatening roar.

'Shove over!' Old Nell pushed at Wally Stubbs to move him further in. There was just room for one more under here, but the girl Bren hadn't come, she never did. Bren was a relative of Old Nell who lived in the scrapyard's old bus with her soldier husband, Uncle Tommy Price, and she took her chance in there. Some chance! Johnnie reckoned – as the sudden shriek of a bomb closed his eyes and shut his mind to what could happen next: the end of everything, the great big black-out.

Grandad swore in his throat and Old Nell took in her breath as if she was holding it ready for talking to God. First the evil noise of the thing coming down, then that wait down here on the receiving end, with no time at all for messing with prayer. The shriek of the bomb became a scream as it neared earth, and the dirt blast suddenly spat into Johnnie's mouth a split second before the shake that seemed to jump the shelter a foot off the ground.

'The devils!'

Followed by the thunderbolt which was a ton of high explosive in the next street. Their caravan shook beside the shelter, and the old bus Bren was in threw its crockery all over the place as the girl screamed her throat raw. Grandad Stubbs' rag-and-bone horse kicked in her stall but she was hitched too tight to damage herself and made a wild screech instead.

'Close!' Which was a whole thank-you speech from Grandad – gratitude for not being the one who'd copped it that time. Old Nell let out her breath, still here on earth in one piece. There was another whistling from the sky but it was a street further off, while up above somewhere the first wave of bombers went on over and dropped their death and destruction on some other poor beggars.

Johnnie let himself go a bit, but he wasn't shifting anywhere till the all-clear sounded to say that the raid was over.

'You all right, Bren?' Old Nell called out in the lull.

There was no answer from the bus – and none expected, because Bren would be shaking under her bed in there and strangling for comfort one of those dolls she called her babies. Poor old Bren! Johnnie had a soft spot for the girl – big enough to be a soldier's wife but with the mind of a kid at Infants' school. She'd never come out and under the shelter because Old Nell would poke her for taking up room with her dolls – and the daft girl wouldn't dream of leaving them behind.

'Hitler's sent a packet for the docks tonight!' Grandad Stubbs muttered, grinding his teeth. 'We'll be stuck here till morning!'

And it was cold under there. Johnnie looked out of the side. Torn pieces of metal from the bombs and shells were still pinging around like snipers' bullets so he wouldn't stick his head out far; but he could see the white beams of the searchlights waving about, trying to illuminate a bomber so the gunners on the ground could get a fix on it.

'Get yourself in, boy!' Old Nell commanded. 'Piece

of that shrapnel flying about could have your head off!' Her words slipped on the loose rub of her gums but she was a tough old nut and you didn't go against her, no one did, not even Uncle Tommy Price. '*And another lot's coming over!*'

Johnnie pulled himself in tight again. And right enough, a new wave of throbbing engines was coming in, even lower this time. Johnnie shut his eyes and tried to think of something else – but there was nothing else in his rotten life that he wanted to think about. It was going to be a long dangerous night.

Half a mile from Stubbs's scrapyard a neat row of Anderson shelters ran down the gardens, every one well dug in with a little sandbagged entrance. Some even had fancy names: Shangri-La and It's-It. The previous summer, before the declaration of war, there had actually been a street competition for the most beautiful garden shelter.

Reg Lewis at 127 hadn't won – and he hadn't wanted to, either. He was an auxiliary fireman, going training after work instead of gardening. So instead of geraniums he'd got himself fifty extra sandbags for the top of his shelter. He'd run out electric light and bought an extra section of corrugated iron for letting their feet stretch out when they slept down there, as he reckoned they would. And this Saturday night, on the Blue Watch rest day, he was at home with Vera and little Shirley – their three-year-old who was sleeping through the bombing.

Reg, with a tin hat on, was near the door of the

shelter on the look-out for incendiaries. But fire-bombs were small stuff, and this raid was a big one. The way the Germans were pasting the London docks, Regional Control would be calling up fire crews from out in the country – plus all the small stuff, the pumps pulled behind taxis, and Morris Eight family cars. And tomorrow, like yesterday, Reg would be scorching his face and frying his eyes at the fires already burning since Thursday.

An ack-ack gun suddenly opened up at the corner of the street, a loud shock among the houses. They were pulling them round London on the backs of lorries so the bomber pilots would think there were more than there really were. The anti-aircraft gun jumped Shirley in her sleep, and she ground her teeth before she settled again.

'We'll get you away to Auntie Lim's on Monday,' Reg said, ducking in. That throaty voice meant he was serious. 'You'll be safe as houses in Hitchin.' Which Vera only grunted at, because houses were crumbling like old cake these nights.

But she did agree with him.

'Putting up with Auntie Lim's no sacrifice, not against . . .' She looked at little Shirley and shivered – when a close whistle had her burying her head, and covering Shirley with her arm.

Most days people went on scrambling to work, because working hard for the War Effort was how Hitler would get beaten. Buses got round the holes where last night's bombs had dropped. People crossed miles of hosepipe which led to the river or the hydrants or the emergency water tanks. Lessons went on where schools were still running, and shops opened up even though they had more shelf than stock.

But today was Sunday and south London was getting the brick dust out of everything and listening to the forces wireless programme and pretending life was normal. Except for people like Grandad Stubbs on the scrap cart, where a bit of business was still going on.

With that old dead stare into her blinkers, the horse clopped her cart along the street and past Sebastopol Road school, Grandad riding a shaft and Johnnie swinging his legs on the tailboard.

'Lum-*ber*, iron lum-*ber*!' The rag-and-bone voice seemed to holler from deep down. Scarf crossed at the throat, cap set back off his ruddy face, Wally Stubbs – 'Fair Prices Paid' – let his voice go, then gave the street a stare. On the look-out for a curtain scraping aside, or an apron waiting in a doorway and a skinny-armed wave, someone wanting to make a sixpence. But a sudden scrambling swayed the cart.

'Oi! You got worms, 'ave you?'

'No, I ain't!'

'Sit still, then. She'll only stop, the mare! Gi'-up!' He flicked his whip at the horse's back.

''Ead down – *school*!' Johnnie shouted it like it was *Unexploded Bomb!*

Wally Stubbs spat. 'Get off! It's Sunday. Anyhow, they're all down the country, e-vac-uated. Got enough on their plate wi'out botherin' over catchin' you.'

Johnnie lifted his head from the rags and looked at the school. London School Board, Sebastopol Road. His grandad was right, it was empty – windows on this side all pushed up shut and a padlock chained on the 'Babies' gate – except that over the fence in the playground there was a grey fire engine, and the shouts of men playing some game with a ball. This school was now a fire station.

Like a dog going from growl to bark, Wally Stubbs filled out his neck again. 'Lum-*ber*, iron lum-*ber*!' – followed by the old dry cough he was all for slaking down the Woodman. 'Casualties, missing persons, the only item they're interested in is keeping their lists up to the mark. You stay in London, boy, an' no attendance men are gonna bother lookin' for you – 'less you're buried under an 'ouse somewhere . . .'

Wally's eyes went back to the terrace still standing, a street with front gardens just wide enough for getting round to clean the windows. Some of them were shut up; some had bomb-damage cracks down the walls; one had its roof covered with tarpaulin; and all of them had windows like old flags, with diagonal crosses of gummed webbing to stop the glass from flying.

Sundays were never much for business, although a wartime Sunday sometimes had its rewards for Wally Stubbs – like a bombed-out house and no one around. But Johnnie had the itch to get finished. He wanted to get back to the yard quick because he wasn't so sure how *e-vac-uated* everyone really was, whatever the old man said. Evacuation meant sending city kids to

13

the safety of the country away from the raids. But the people who made sure you were in school somewhere – the School Board Attendance men – they weren't all down the country, sure as eggs – and Johnnie knew some who'd kick a kid's dead body for a sign of life if they thought they'd get a result, Sunday, Monday or Good Friday.

Johnnie sniffed. 'Rabbit. That'll do me.' He dangled and swung his legs off the tailboard again like any Sunday boy helping out – because you had to look the part. The worst picture you could give was someone on the run, eyes everywhere and feet ready to scarper away.

And Johnnie *was* on the run, big time. He spat like his grandad at the thought of the place he was running from, the Approved School where they put the juvenile offenders, the young crooks – and where they'd put Johnnie Stubbs. And he spat at the thought of the people from the town hall, the Juvenile Court officials who'd got him so wrong. He wasn't a thief, he wasn't a looter who fed off someone else's misery by stealing their stuff when their houses were bombed. He was East End, he was tough, but Johnnie Stubbs was as straight as a carrot. That gold watch was his, legitimate.

With his old dad off the scene, called up in the army, his second-hand shop shut up till he came marching home again, Johnnie hadn't had anyone to defend him: no one to tell the Juvenile Court the truth. And without the court Johnnie could have lived easy with Old Nell and his grandad, all above board, no problem. Instead of which, innocent, clean as a whistle, the rotten Juvenile had sent him down – away to the approved school they called *HMS Greengates*, the big old house dressed up as a ship – and into the hands of headmaster 'Captain' Rosewarn and his cat-o'-nine-tails crew who'd as soon give you a beating as give you breakfast.

His dad had been right. 'Deal in second-hand and they treat you second-rate.' Because they didn't do to the likes of Johnnie Stubbs what they did to war orphans, they didn't find you foster parents or distant relatives or proper schools – if there was a whiff off you that you lived on your wits they slung you in with the delinquents, all those older boys who knew just where to boot you to make you fetch up.

Not that he was any yellowbelly. It took three to get him down as a rule; and he could hump any man's load out on the round with Grandad. He looked back at the half-cart of roped-up scrap. They hadn't done bad today, either: with the bath they'd told the old girl wouldn't mend, the brass bedstead off the bomb site, and those bits of plumber's pipe. No, they'd done well – *and* done it without Uncle Tommy, so he couldn't go on that the boy was useless, no more than a begging mouth.

'Lum-*ber*, iron lum-*ber*!'

Just so long as he could keep himself clear of anyone looking to make trouble for the Stubbses; and so long as Uncle Tommy's daft Brenda didn't sound off her mouth.

He looked up at the turrets of Sebastopol Road as

the school backed off round a corner. No different, schools weren't, this side of the river from where he lived, on the other. The same shouts from the teachers, the same yellow rulers across your knuckles. But weren't they like halls of paradise, compared to *HMS Greengates* and the animals who worked there?

Inside Sebastopol Road School Reg Lewis, with his fireman's trousers on, was lying on his bed staring up at a classroom ceiling. Back from three hours in the docks, Blue Watch was being held in reserve, but they'd done their maintenance on the Dennis fire engine and Reg didn't fancy volleyball. Reg was local – he'd started school and left school in this same building – and he'd long ago in days of peace stared at this very ceiling, looking for answers which wouldn't come. No difference. He got up and wandered over to a window, saw the playground shelter where two fire engines the regulars called appliances stood tight together, like insects in a nest, staring out. Sunday, and him on watch instead of sitting down to a last dinner with Vera and little Shirley. God, he was going to miss them when they went off to the country tomorrow.

Up the road, Vera would be racing the clock, packing, while in here time was hanging like a poetry lesson. He fished out a rub of Digger Plug tobacco and stuffed a pipe, walked out of the classroom and under the badminton net strung across the hall. He'd have a chat with the girls in the Watch Room. He put a match to his pipe bowl, and saw the King of England looking out at him from his picture on the wall. Caught smoking in the school hall by George VI! The pipe made more smoke and he waved it away, danced it up towards the ceiling girders. Who'd ever have had children if they'd known there'd be another war? But then, imagine life without little Shirley . . .

For Shirley every night was still a novelty, going to bed out in the garden, the oil lamp flickering over all her toys, with her mum on the opposite bunk, reading stories out of the 'Pip, Squeak and Wilfred' annual till her voice got croaky quiet. But Shirley knew this wasn't the way things were supposed to be. She was only three – and she was scared of the sound of the air raid siren because it started up like a dog going to howl, and its wail when it got going curdled her inside. But she liked the searchlights shining up on the clouds; and she had names for the big silver elephant balloons which dipped and swayed, going up, coming down, puffing in and out. Her daddy came home in his two rows of silver buttons, and he sometimes slept in the shelter with them – so the war was fun as well. And she turned down her mouth that Sunday when she saw the big suitcase out for going away.

'Don't want to go to Auntie Lim.'

'Sssh!' She got a kiss. 'We'll have old "Pip, Squeak and Wilfred" with us, eh?'

There was a ritual for everything, and the annual was part of it. Shirley had to have things done the same way in the right order every time, even going down the shelter to sleep. While she stood in her dressing gown at the back door watching, her mother would run across the garden to the Anderson shelter. The red glow of the stove would be blown out and the little lamp would be lit, smelling like a grocer's shop that sold paraffin. Every night the same. Then it would be Shirley's turn. The dolls to sit on the concrete shelf would be carried out, then a quick run back for the final trip – Shirley's mother with a hot-water bottle and Shirley with the annual cuddled in her arm.

It made Vera cry that Sunday night, carrying her child out into that shelter. 'Thank God we're away to the country, Babe. No more of this.' And Shirley was tucked up in the long bunk, cramped for space by her dolls and enjoying the grown-up sheets which stretched down for ever past her feet.

'Story in a bit, eh?'

'Pip, Squeak and Wilfred!'

'What else? Mum's just gonna sort out for five more minutes. Won't be far . . .' Vera gave the girl a back-soon kiss.

Shirley's thumb went in. 'Curtain open.'

'Yeah, Hitler won't see your little lamp.' Hitler not being Adolf but old Johnson, the air-raid warden from over the road who was always on the alert for anyone showing a light in the black-out. Vera backed out of the shelter and pulled the heavy black curtain wide open so that Shirley could see the kitchen door from her bunk. 'Not long, promise . . .'

'We won't go asleep.'

'Five minutes.' And Vera went into the house, a quick look back from the kitchen door. And she *would* only be five minutes, because she'd never broken a promise in her life.

'Pull that curtain across! You want the law round?' Wally Stubbs's face was lit up angry by the light spilling from the single-decker bus in the yard. He thumped on its side and made the dog bark. 'Can't you get it into your thick 'ead – keep that curtain across!'

Tommy Price's face came to the window and stared out. But he said nothing, just jerked the black curtain across.

Inside, the girl was crying. She cried morning, noon and night, Brenda the cousin-wife. And any sudden shouting would have her in a corner with her fingers in her ears. Pricey looked at her and swore. 'Don't you start!' he warned. He picked up the dirty-faced doll she'd dropped and threw it on the bed. 'Get me a cup o' tea an' shut up!'

Brenda did what she was told. Sixteen and a bit, she always did what the soldier said. She tipped water from a cracked jug into a saucepan and set it on the camping stove. Not a word, but when the mug was in her husband's hand she grabbed for the doll and clutched it back to her skinny chest.

'What you want with that thing?'

Brenda was rocking, crooning quietly to the doll, her dirty golden hair round its head. 'My baby,' she said. 'Bren's baby.'

Pricey looked at her and his hard face said it all.

19

The doll would be the only baby she'd have while he was sober. 'Scuddin' war!' he said. 'Scuddin' prisoner, I am, with you . . .' He slapped his mug down and started fingering in pots and bowls till he came out with a coin, a two-bob bit he'd hidden. 'I'm over the Woodman,' he told her. He pushed open the door, thought of something else and came back to twist the doll out of her hands. 'While you clear up this stinkin' mess!' And, after slapping her for screaming, he slammed out of the bus and made it rock, slinging the doll somewhere into the scrap for spite.

Johnnie watched him go. Behind the tethered horse in her stall, he saw no more than a vague shape in the dark, but his brain saw clear as day there was going to be trouble with Uncle Tommy Price before too long, real trouble. Old Nell would only take so much against Brenda before she went for the man, the layabout, not humping his weight of the work. But Johnnie understood Uncle Tommy, a bit of him, anyway, because they were both on the run: him from the approved school and Pricey from the military police, the Red Caps. Except Johnnie was going to do more than hide all the time. He was going back home to Woodseer Street over Aldgate when he could, going to get some evidence about that gold watch. While Tommy Price had no hope. You couldn't keep your head down for ever, and Pricey looked like he was ready to blow. Which bothered Johnnie, because if it happened in a big way and the law got called to sort it, he'd soon get found himself. And that was something he couldn't even think about. Back to *HMS*

Greengates, over Essex. He rubbed at his backside, remembering. He had lines across his bum you could write music on. So it was to keep the peace and no great love for daft Brenda that had him scrambling over a pile of junk where Pricey had chucked the doll.

He reckoned it had gone over the old iron, some-where near the rag – rust and sharp edges on the one side and that old soft stink on the other – but he'd got to clamber and get it; and be quick about it. There was no way must Brenda start screaming again and bring some Nosy Parker round the yard. His fingers and feet felt their way in the gloom, the way he'd got over the fences and walls from the approved school. And it made him think – on account of everything made him think – of that last swearing his head off at 'Captain' Rosewarn, and the cane, a double, with him held down over a vaulting horse in the gym. Sweating on a dark night, and a climb up the wire fence where his boy's hands and toes had just fitted into the wobbly holes. Followed by a two-day walk back to London, just a bit of dodging, and the ferry across the river to his grandad's yard; forgetting Woodseer Street for a bit, because that was the first place they'd look, wasn't it? His old home. Sure as eggs.

He raked over the pile. Rusted bits slid under his boots and sharp edges cut at his hands. But what he saw on this side was all iron and hard, and among the stink of the rags on the other everything was torn and soft, nothing in between, no rubber, no doll. He climbed and slipped, held his breath, scared that his boots might bury the doll for ever. He swore. As the moon got up, weird shadows grew in the rags, so seeing a doll dressed in rags itself was like looking for a pint of water in a river. He'd have to leave it and wait till the morning.

He sat on the rags, spat into them and swore again. He'd had this bad feeling since they'd passed that school today. The feeling of *them* being about. Getting close. The beaters. So why the hell couldn't the army have written? Why couldn't they say where his dad was? It only needed his word for everything to get sorted out a treat, to make being here with Old Nell all on the level . . . As it was, right now Johnnie was on a real sharp edge, with Pricey coming back from the pub tanked up and Brenda in there all up the wall. Any rotten thing could happen to him.

2

THE ALERT had gone from yellow to red, the air-raid warnings had been sounded and Blue Watch waited for the first call-out of the night to come through.

Reg Lewis sat with the rest, who'd all gone quiet in the fire station shelter, their minds on their families. It was the docks getting it again tonight and any moment could bring Regional Control on the blower and a blacked-out ride under the Thames. But at least over the docks wasn't Plumstead and his girls – a selfish, wicked thought.

The first they heard of the Heinkel bomber was a low drone coming in across the rooftops, an engine sputtering and dying and pumping out oil, where the ack-ack boys had scored a hit. And in a count of three it was on them, almost low enough to take the bell off the school roof, everyone diving for the floor; chased hard by an explosion, as if the plane had crashed into the next street. Blast blew them about like sticks in a whirlwind as they heard school windows smashed in, and the shout to go. Running out to the playground they spat brick dust and splinters – and still got the fire engine out through the gates in two minutes.

Up in the cab Reg buckled and buttoned with the

rest, mouth tight, trying not to think: because, *Flaxton Road, top end* had been the call as they'd run for the sheds. He wriggled his axe belt into place and stared out through the front. It wouldn't be true, would it – that red in the sky over where he lived? Not with them off to the country tomorrow? A house or so either way could make all the difference, and distances were hard to judge. His eyes hurt with the staring, and his ears didn't hear when the others suddenly went quiet around him, only what was in his head: 'Please, God, not my girls! Not my girls!' But as the windscreen ran into a sudden cloud of dust and the wheels started bumping over debris he saw the first people running about, and he yelled and pushed over to count the rooftops – and he saw where the end one, the corner house, his roof, wasn't there any more.

The rubble covered the road feet deep and people were climbing towards the burning heap where the house had been. An air-raid warden with a stirrup pump and a bucket was going at it, others were scrabbling in the bricks and tatters of curtain and bits of bedding. But there was no aeroplane tail fin, no fuselage; it hadn't been the Heinkel, but one of its bombs.

The appliance stopped, the crew jumped out, orders were shouted by the leading fireman: 'Pump to work from hydrant! Unreel hoses!' The driver pushed Reg away. They could do without the poor blighter while he went to find out.

People shouted.

'Reg!'

'We haven't seen 'em!'

'They *was* down the shelter?'

Somehow Reg ran straight; somehow he put one foot in front of the other and kept his balance, hands on hot bricks, a boot on his flattened bedroom door. He shouted. 'Vera! *Vera!*' A whistle blew and every-one fell quiet to listen for any faint reply. But every-one knew already. If Vera Lewis and the little girl weren't in the shelter, there wasn't much chance they were still alive. It had been a direct hit, right down through the house, with the crater in the foundations and the rest caved in on top. Blue Watch knocked down the fire within minutes. Then people stood, lis-tened; Reg scrabbled, but he knew where they ought to be, too. It was that shelter buried under slate and brick and timber that concerned him now, how well it had stood up to the fall on it, and what the shock waves might have done under the ground.

Lining up on a lamppost, Reg worked out where the shelter entrance should be. The iron washing mangle kept out at the back had been thrown like a toy on to the mound, but within seconds his crew had cleared it and the neighbours were there with him, bare hands and shovels and buckets, helping to dig the Lewis girls out. No wasted words. 'Over here!' or 'Ease it!' until they cleared the top of the entrance, a hole just big enough for Reg to get through. Another whistle blew and they stopped the appliance engine. Dead silence. Reg didn't pause. He took the rescue lamp which someone pushed into his hand and went head-first into the shelter. 'Vera! Shirley! You all right? Say something, girl, say something!' He shone the light round the small space. Bedclothes all over, garden dirt everywhere, but the roof had held. He stared harder than for anything ever in his life, knowing too well how small and scrappy a huddled human being could be. 'Vera!' But, nothing. Pulling himself right in, balancing between the bunks, he let his heavy feet down carefully and started lifting eiderdowns and blankets and pillows. But there was no one there; and in a sudden awful emptiness he turned to the faces crowded in the hole and reported in his fireman's voice, 'Area clear, no casualties here.' Only when the faces had gone did he curl himself down between the bunks and start to cry.

Shirley hadn't felt the quake as the bomb exploded and she hadn't heard the bang. Wrapped in sleep, she had bounced on her bunk and woken only when the blast of air rushed in and the bedclothes flew around her. She came to enough to see the red sky flickering in on what had happened. She was all on her own, and everything was upside-down, with dirt all over the bunks. She opened her mouth and screamed for her mum, and she kicked to get her romper legs out from the tangle of bedclothes. She screamed and she shouted, and she crawled along the bunk towards the red sky. But when she put her head outside she couldn't see where her mum and the house were any more. Where her back door had been, and her back wall, and everything she knew, all that was left was a pile of knocked-down bricks and a big fire burning.

'Mum! Mummy!' Shirley screamed again, and in her rompers and dressing gown she ran for her mother the only way she could, out where the fence and back gate had been and into the street at the side; just seconds before the back wall of next door came crashing down across her garden.

A third time Shirley screamed. She stood in the crackle and the smoke and the dust – her feet apart, her small fists clenched tight and her head thrown back – to screech in terror for her mother. But her mother didn't come, and she didn't call out to say that everything was all right, either. In panic Shirley ran to where she thought she'd be, gone up the street to Auntie Palmer's for something. She hurt her feet on broken brick and glass, was lost in a cloud of dust, twisting, turning, running round a corner away from some men shouting – until, when the air was suddenly clear, all she could see was a row of houses she didn't know, all different walls, and at the end of it the start of somewhere else.

She ran. She didn't know where she was running, except her mum always came round the next corner, was always there all the time really. Big guns banged and things fell about and aeroplanes made their noises, and she screamed for a while in the din. And then she was screamed out, with no idea in the world where she was going, just running to where her mum would suddenly scoop her up. Her ragged feet trotted her across a road and round a corner, then up and down more white kerbs, trying to see her proper house again; while all the time the houses were getting bigger and the fields were beginning, and she was coming to where the dried-up Quaggy river ran. Here the road turned into cinders, patchy and pot-holed, and there were flattened ruts where cart-wheels went.

It was a corrugated gate that stopped her: where the track ran out it was crossed by a tall gate with a lock and chain. Not going back, Shirley pushed against it while her legs shook. Was her mum behind here, playing hide-and-seek? She pushed again, and the gate gave a foot – and Shirley half fell and half tottered into the scrapyard. And there she saw a bus. Could it be the bus going to take them to Auntie Lim's, with her mum inside it getting the tickets?

Out of the bus came a big girl with a coat on, crying at the ground.

'My baby! Bren's baby out in the bombs!'

'Shut up, an' dowse that light!' Now an old lady was shouting, somewhere round a corner.

'Bren's coming!' the big girl called out. 'Where's Bren's baby?' She took a step or two, looking up and down, and Shirley saw her eyes blinking in the red glow. She pulled the coat about, looked this side and that, and then she was looking straight at Shirley.

'My baby!' the big girl shouted, and she came over and picked her up and carried her into the bus. And Shirley went with her, warm and cuddled, because she was being taken to where her mum was . . .

There was a rattle at the corrugated gate. 'Oi! Put that light out! Who's in there?' It was a loud voice, and the sort that had to get answered.

'Who wants to know?'

'Police.'

'There's a raid over my 'ead, dunno about over yours!' Old Nell came out from under the home-made shelter.

'Someone showing a light.'

'She lost the run of the cat. It won't show no more.' The old woman and the policeman in his steel helmet faced each other through the gap in the gate.

'Better not. Who lives in there, anyway?' He was eyeing the bus.

'Niece. Not all there.' Old Nell tapped her forehead.

'Then you want to keep an eye on her. Light still shows up above, whether she's all there or not.'

'I'll watch her.'

'I'll come round and tell her myself, tomorrow. Bit of uniform usually frightens 'em.'

An ack-ack battery suddenly opened up across the fields in Welling, following a plane pinned in a searchlight, somewhere out over the Thames.

'Get yourself in, you've got no tin hat.' And the policeman went. But he'd kept looking about him all the way, and he'd dropped a bomb of his own. Old Nell went back towards her shelter, thumping hard on the side of the bus. 'Here that, you daft ha'p'orth? He's coming back tomorrow!' And she suddenly swore and changed direction and went back into her caravan instead.

In the Woodman the beer was weak and gassy, out of bottles because the brewery horses had just been evacuated to the country. But a raid gave any old drink an edge, and the people who braved it out in a pub weren't going to let their evening seem wasted: least of all Tommy Price, on the run. And by now he'd had more than enough of the weak stuff to make up any difference. Red-faced and shirt hanging out, he was spinning the yarn of his war wound to a dressed-up woman who kept on about rubbing it better. The window curtains were backed with black, there was a collecting box on the counter for Salute the Soldier Week, and slipped slates had clattered into the men's urinal from the blast of the last bomb; otherwise there was this great pretence that nothing was any different from peacetime.

Including Old Nell coming swinging in. She pushed open the door like a regular and spotted Pricey, straight off. Pricey stared her out.

'Outside!' she said.

'Hello, this the missus?' the ladyfriend asked, dabbing the gin from her lipstick.

But Pricey hadn't time to swat the insult. He was fighting through the black door drapes and outside quicker than Old Nell could turn round. 'Red Caps?' he wanted to know, his eyes up and down the street.

'Just as bad!'

They pulled back into a doorway as the Welling ack-ack opened up again.

'Rozzer, been nosing. Coming back tomorrow.'

'Serious?'

30

'Enough to get me out in this without my best drawers!'

'What you reckon?'

They ran a couple of doorways further on as distant explosions cracked. Above their heads the searchlights were turning night into day, sweeping the sky and making mountain ranges of the clouds. The barrage balloons were high, forcing the raiders higher and less accurate, so a stray stick of bombs could come their way as easy as the docks', like the night before.

'He'll come back. That policeman was bloodhounding the yard for something not right. And he had that look said he'd find it.'

'I can make myself scarce.' Pricey's bottles of bravery stank on his breath, and his knees went, as if he might sit on a doorstep.

'What about her? You'll make Bren scarce, won't you?' Old Nell came out and braved the sky before he would. 'She'll mouth you off to anyone.'

'Blast her!' Pricey let the old woman go first, in case the police were round the next corner. He caught up. 'I can't just do a run, won't get far if they're looking for me serious . . .'

Old Nell stopped, pushed him hard against a brick wall. 'Then you get off with the old bus. Take it. Get on the road. Go to Dukes's site, lose yourself down the country.'

'Dukes's? I'm not a gippo.'

'There's enough gypsy blood in Brenda to pass, an' you're married to her, aren't you?'

He kicked at a pig bin chained to a lamppost, hurt his foot because it was full and heavy with the street's scrap food.

'You know where it is?'

He swore. Of course he did: he'd had to stand in front of old Dukesey Joyce to get gypsy permission for Bren to marry him.

'Get off now in all this. There's enough on their plate without you. An' something else –' She was dragging him now, by the shirtfront. 'Take the boy along o' you, or they'll soon nose him out. We get a visit and it ain't gonna be long before they put Stubbs together with Stubbs.'

'What?' But Pricey was suddenly being sick in the gutter.

'Gawd! Give you a sniff of the barmaid's apron . . .'

He retched again, pulled himself up on her. 'If I'm sick, you old crow, it ain't that beer, I tell you. It's getting married quick to put off the call-up. Fat lot of good that done!'

Old Nell wasn't listening; she ran across a road, looking up instead of left and right.

'You hear? A clever job you done there, getting the daft cow married!' And he was sick again, spewing as he doubled to catch her up. 'But she'd better take a turn for the best, I tell you!'

Up the road where the bomb had dropped they had found Vera Lewis and were pulling her out of the rubble. Heavy Rescue had come, and while Reg was led away with bleeding hands they had taken over. They knew how houses were built and how they fell, they knew about the different sorts of bombs and they knew how blast worked, where the likely places were for buried people to be – and whether they could expect to find somebody all in one piece, or with bits of them scattered over the district. In battledress and dungarees they worked with heavy lifting gear to move the big stuff, but first they went at it with their whistles for silence and their careful hands.

And it was a hand they uncovered first, at the rear of the rubble where the kitchen had been: a hand, then an arm, then a shoulder; and thank God all joined together. No one said too much till Reg had been taken into Auntie Palmer's for a cup of tea, but they went on working like archaeologists to find the head. Hearth brushes and fine trowels, but mostly delicate fingers finally uncovered a strangely peaceful face: smothered and filled with dust and debris, in the nose and the ears, and the mouth a choke of blood and powdered brick. Oxygen was called for, and while the Heavy Rescue officer laid himself across the casualty, his men shored up a smoking architrave which was holding back a section of dangerous wall. Up the rubble came a Civil Defence doctor who cleared her mouth and tested with the cold steel of a stethoscope tube for the unlikely sign of breathing. And a shout went up for 'Stretcher party!' when he twisted his head to report that she was alive. And an angry yell from Heavy Rescue to take ruddy care – there could be a baby underfoot as well.

Reg went with Vera in the ambulance while the

search went on in the ruins for Shirley. He sat and held her cold hand and watched as more oxygen was given, and he cleaned her face with a handkerchief and water from the ambulance flask. She was covered in yellow brick dust like a figure rolled in custard powder, and she was still, very still.

He looked up at the ambulance woman.

'Depends on her internal injuries,' she said. 'She's only just alive . . .' There was never any room for false hope.

Reg nodded, swallowed. He looked back at his wife. 'Vera, Vera . . .' And fireman or not, he was crying again, and moaning in his throat, and looking out of the back window to what they were leaving behind.

The ambulance passed the junction of Flaxton Road and Kirkham Street on its way to St Nicholas's Hospital. It made another vehicle stop short, something with old slow brakes and wonky steering.

'What's a bus doing out this time of night? On the soup run?' But the ambulance woman didn't care really, and Reg certainly didn't, as he cradled Vera's head and tried to warm some life into her hands.

In the bus, Johnnie Stubbs looked out through the front passenger window. He'd been told to keep down so he didn't show too much of himself. Ambulance! *Touch your collar never swallow till you see a dog.* That was the lucky saying when you saw one of them. He pulled himself down under the blanket again and tried to go with the bumps. It was an old

Leyland bus they were in, the sort of single-decker you saw down the country. The driver's cab was separate, he got in it from outside, and there was a leather blind to stop the light shining through; except tonight they had no lights on. Well, at least he didn't have to look at the sweating back of Tommy Price, driving like he was going to stop for nothing. And nobody to talk to in here because Bren had tucked down under her bedclothes before he'd got in, hugging a big doll, by the look of that lump under there. Every corner they went round some item fell off a table or a cupboard or the sink – no one had reckoned the bus would be swerving round corners tonight.

Johnnie rested an elbow on the decking and swore at the webbed-over windows. What a turn-out! Being forced by Old Nell to bung his bits into a haversack and go down the country. It was his home in Woodseer Street, over Aldgate, he wanted to get to – when the heat was off. Find some evidence to clear his name. Find out where his dad was posted, who knew? Anyway, what was good about the country round London? Too close to *HMS Greengates*, all of it. The night he'd got out he'd wanted himself dead, and he'd have taken running head-first into a machine-gun rather than the swipe of that stick any more. Finding Wally Stubbs, his gone-away grandad, had been his target. At least he was family; and the old bloke did seem to like him. A rough idea of the address, a bit of asking around, and most people in Plumstead knew Stubbs's horse and cart – and then the old man had taken him on like he owed him something.

'Where's your dad?'

'Called up.'

'Where's your mum?'

'Never had one.'

'No, nor you never. What you up to?'

'On the run from approved school.'

'What for?'

'Told you, my dad's called up . . .'

'And?'

'They found this gold watch down my sock.'

'Stupid little blighter!'

And that had been it. Old Nell had given him a bit of cheese and sauce and he'd been in; and it had been like helping his dad over Aldgate on the stall all over again. Customers never looked twice at a kid out of school when there was a horse and cart or a barrow about. But getting shunted off with Tommy Price and daft Bren, going God knew where, this was different again. And dangerous.

He stared at the bus roof while the air raid crashed around. What was a bus made of anyhow? It looked like wood on the inside, and a thin bit of tin with a coat of old paint on the outside; and what would that stop? Guns were going off all along the railway, and you could hear the bombs hitting the docks as if they were in the next street. It was like being out in it without anything to save you, and any second could have Johnnie Stubbs in bits all over the shop.

Johnnie sat himself up. He was known as tough over Aldgate. It was only the bigger kids ever wanted to fight him, and he could get what he wanted mostly by staring his eyes and showing his fist or rolling his sleeve. He'd always bleed before he'd cry, and he'd never had a kiss in his life. But for all that, tonight he was scared, and it was a lot more than the bombs.

Pricey gave the gearbox a grinding, getting out of an incendiary hole; he sorted out a gear and jerked the bus on. A saucepan fell off a nail and must have hit Bren.

'Get off! Ow! Mind my baby!'

Her and her stupid pretend baby! By the weird red and yellow light coming in from the sky, Johnnie could see her sitting up. She hadn't been asleep, or anything like; as she came up her face had a wide-awake look about it. She rubbed her shoulder, the way kids do, crying worse than they're hurt.

'Who done that?'

'Pot fell off.'

'Stupid pot!' She looked round, as if she was clocking for the first time that they were on the move. 'Where are we? We *going*?'

A street gun went off, rocked the bus and rattled it through. It made Johnnie jump, duck down; but Bren didn't move, went on staring at him. 'You don't live in here!'

'Do now.'

'Bren and her baby live in here.'

'Yeah, that's right. And Tommy Price, and now Uncle Johnnie!' The poor loony cow – Johnnie stared her out, trying to look on the bright side himself, but hell's bells, what was it going to be like living with her and that runaway soldier, a man who'd do for the pair of them rather than get copped by the Red Caps!

'Well, Uncle Johnnie shut his eyes,' Bren said. 'Go on! Mummy's going to feed the baby.'

'Don't talk pills! You ain't got no real baby.'

Even so, Bren was sitting up in the bed and starting to pull up her jumper.

'Behave yourself, I don't want to see what you got!' But she'd pulled her old jumper right up and was showing something that didn't seem much different from what Johnnie looked like.

'Watch out for Pricey, he'll kill you, showing yourself off!' Johnnie warned. The bus had slowed down for some reason, and that folding leather down the back of the driver's inside window had a little hole in it for looking through. If Tommy Price thought they were up to something in here he'd come round and hurt the both of them both worse than *HMS Green-gates*. 'Put yourself away, will you!'

But she wasn't with him. She had a funny look in her eyes which was wild and peaceful both at once, and she was pulling under the bedclothes to get up one of her dolls. Gordon Bennett, this was *mad* mad! And now the bus had stopped. Johnnie pulled at his own rag of a blanket and went to lie down again, didn't want to look. He was going to keep his head right down on account of all sorts going to happen now. But his last look as he went to hide himself away had him coming back up quicker than a jack-in-the-box.

Because up from under her bedclothes Bren was pulling not a doll, not even a life-size doll, but a real, live, yawning little kid. A girl. She pulled her up towards herself.

'Bren! Strewth! Good God alive, what you got there?' He couldn't believe what he was seeing, couldn't have blinked if he'd had salt thrown in his face.

'Bren's baby.'

Eyes out of his head, he watched her nuzzle the little girl, very awkward, pushing her face to her scrappy chest.

Just as the cab door slammed outside. The bus had been stopped for a bit now and Tommy Price was coming round. Johnnie jumped up, then threw himself down again. He'd be asleep. Dead to the wide. He couldn't be into this if he was asleep, could he? There was a thump on the side of the bus as Pricey demanded to be let in: a double thump, and then another, the man not risking his voice. And Johnnie screwed his eyes as his brain racked. Because Tommy Price would just chuck them out, all of them. Air raids going on, no Old Nell to check any more, it'd be easy – and that man wasn't going back to the army to face locking up, not for anyone. And what was a baby girl going to do for their chances?

'Open up, will you? You deaf in there?' It was shouted softly, but with a great thump to rock the bus. Strong, he was. And Bren, sitting up, was stroking this kid's hair, with a look on her face which said she was as happy as anyone could ever be.

'Let him in, then,' she said, 'Uncle Johnnie. He can kiss the baby night-night.'

3

THEY WERE run off their feet at St Nick's. Two doctors were taking a quick look at ambulance casualties out in the front yard so that the Brought in Deads could be sent direct to the mortuary down at Plumstead Baths. Inside, doctors, nurses and orderlies were going everywhere at a run, dodging round people who were sitting and lying and nursing themselves in shock. No one had slept for two days and nights. Their voices were loud and croaky. They didn't bother with whole sentences any more. But in all the scramble there was very little noise. Only the children cried. Otherwise, people sat silent and patient, waiting to be seen: like the old woman who was holding a Holiday in Wales tea towel to her head wound, and the air-raid warden, still in his tin hat, who was clutching his arm close to his body as if it might fall off if he let it go. The raid was still going on, the bedridden were in wards on the ground floor and everyone who could be moved was down in the basement shelter. But up here in Casualty there was a feeling that they'd all been hit once. There couldn't be any worse to come, could there?

Through the main doors came Vera Lewis, carried by two stretcher-bearers, alongside them the ambulance woman holding the oxygen mask and Reg

Lewis lugging the canister. They were waved straight into a cubicle where a body had just been lifted away. One of the doctors from outside followed them in at a run, carrying on the examination he'd begun, even before she was on the trolley and the stretcher poles slid away. A nursing sister joined them, a big woman, strong on calm.

'On to the ward, insulin, half oxygen, fifteen-minute check,' the doctor told her. 'Comatose and I don't know what else.' Come back from retirement, he was out of breath and could almost have been a casualty himself. He looked at Reg in his grimy face and uniform, shrugged his shoulders.

'This is her husband, Doctor,' the ambulance woman told him.

'Ah! Good luck, then, son.'

The ambulance woman kissed Reg on the forehead, squeezed his arm and went as well: back to the streets and the next shout. Reg undid the throat hook of his tunic and suddenly looked off duty.

'She was under the house,' he told the sister. 'They're still looking for our little girl.'

The sister was all fingers, hands and arms at the patient, a deft touch. She didn't look round. 'I'll pray to Our Lady.'

'Comatose . . .?' Reg shuffled his feet.

'He's sayin' she's in a coma. If she stays alive the next hour they'll start looking for any obvious internals . . .' Already, she was feeling up and down the legs, then scratching the soles of Vera's feet with a sharp little stick, looking at the face.

Something whistled near and there was a second's halt; then a rumble which had the lampshades swinging.

'You can sit with her on the ward.'

Reg turned towards the flap in the curtain, twisted back again.

'You'll do no earthly good back at the incident. Leave your daughter now. Be of some use to me, will you?'

Reg looked at her, but she was on her way out, heading for a little boy being carried towards her in a woman's arms: a child who was still alive. The fireman found a chair, pulled it in towards the trolley and started saying a prayer he'd learned at school.

Half a mile up the road Heavy Rescue and the Civil Defence supervisor were shaking their heads. There was no sign of the daughter. They had searched around the spot where Vera had been found and then worked their way outwards and downwards into the crater itself. False alarms had been given when clothing was found, and again when two little arms had poked up through the rubble. But it hadn't been Shirley, only a doll.

'No trace, guv.' That was it. Heavy Rescue were packing up, going to the next call-out.

'Blown to smithereens, poor little cock.' It happened: the CD supervisor had had an air-raid warden reported 'simply disappeared' the night before. 'There wouldn't have been much of her to start with, and if the bomb had taken her down with it . . .

'She'll have to go Unaccounted For.'

'Something like that.'

Neighbours stood in a huddle across the road, coats over their shoulders like dressing gowns, heads in scarves and flat caps, the odd saucepan held up for protection. Some of them were ready to sneak in and move brick from brick when there was just a policeman left on duty; they'd easily get round him if there was a skinny chance for the child. And one or two were eyeing the furniture in the empty house next door.

'They were going down the country tomorrow.'

'Fate, i'n't it?'

'If a bomb's got your name on it . . .'

The hoses were being reeled, the fire engine reversed into the side street, and a cordon was going up, tied across the road from one tree to another.

A policeman had a first go at moving the small crowd, the CD supervisor pulled out a notebook and a pencil, looked for a dispatch rider; Blue Watch returned to the cab of the Dennis appliance, one man short.

'What a bloody dirty way to fight a war,' someone said.

The bus was still stopped and Pricey was thumping at the door. Johnnie was twisting all ways, trying to think where to be when he let the man in. Bren, in her own world, was all over the baby.

'Where you off to?' But it was a different voice from outside, not Pricey's.

'Who wants to know?' The thumping stopped.

Johnnie stared again from the two in the bed to the bus door.

'You won't get through here. Oil bomb's hit a gas main up the road.'

Johnnie crawled to the window, lifted the black curtain and looked out. It was hard to see through the grime, but he could make out a white tin hat: probably a warden.

'I'll back up, then, and go round the side streets.'

'Bit big this, isn't it? You on the move?' Johnnie saw the warden walking down the side of the bus, one of those nosy beggars who loved their little armbands.

'Wouldn't you be, with your wife expecting?'

'Night-time?'

'Got the shaded lights.'

'I'd go by daylight, myself.'

'Well, that's you, isn't it?'

Johnnie came away from the window, looked at Bren, who'd started feeling about down in the bed, was putting that look on which said she was opening her mouth for a scream.

'Sssh!' Johnnie ran down the bus, was ready to clamp Bren's mouth if it came to it. But the next he heard was the slam of the cab, and a jerk into reverse which cracked Bren's head and woke the kid. They bumped back over something and she started to cry, then they swung forward round a corner which half threw the pair of them out of the bed.

Someone thumped the side of the bus as they pulled away faster, a cup fell and smashed, and the kid shouted. Bren swore and pulled her jumper down, and Johnnie lost his balance and banged his head on the foot of the stove. He swore. Now they were really moving, given it was only an old bus, the engine going like a Messerschmitt in a power dive. The black-out curtain was flapping about, a cupboard door banged itself open and bits of food and old plates fell out. The bus sides creaked with the sway and the strain, and only with a grip like Old Nell's and not caring about cracking his knees could Johnnie get up, rubbing at his head.

Bren was shouting something, the kid was screaming now, and Johnnie had to hold tight for his life while Bren got her mouth round words he could hear.

'She's wet the bed! This little madam's wet the bed!' And she started shaking the kid as if she'd have her head off.

'What you doing? Leave her!' Johnnie was thrown on to the bed, anyway.

'All wet! Erk! Feel that!' She grabbed at his arm.

But Johnnie didn't fancy getting a hand down in the ruck of Bren's bed. And the kid was all over him now, thinking he was some sort of rescue, had her arms tight round his neck, screaming for her mum.

'All right, all right!' He took her away from Bren and the bed, down towards the back of the bus where he could balance her between the sink and the top of the stove.

'Naughty girl! Mummy cross with naughty girls!' Bren was throwing off the old covers, showing the damp place and sniffing at her fingers. 'Erk! Wee-wees! Wee-wees.' Her voice had gone into a sort of chant. 'Mummy cross with naughty girls.' She raised the back of her hand at them.

The little girl saw her, and still had her arms tight round Johnnie's neck. Her feet, poking out through torn and dirty rompers, were climbing up around him.

'All right, you're all right.' He tried to rock. 'You got a wet bum, that's all.' He snuggled her close to him, staring over her shoulder as he went on saying a load of old nonsense.

But where the hell had Bren got a kid from? What *was* this little girl doing here? Like his dad said, the next song'd be a dance! There was no clue in Bren, stripping the bottom sheet off, spreading a grubby towel in its place. The child in his arms quietened a bit, got heavy as Johnnie went on staring at his barmy cousin, who was sorting herself out now, combing her long scraggy hair, pulling her frock and jumper straight and putting her bare feet into a pair of too-big heeled shoes. She was like a kid dressing up and playing at mothers.

'There wasn't no need to hurt 'er. Bet you piss the bed all the time.'

'Shut yours!'

'She's only a little girl.'

'So? Little girls have to learn. Mummies have to learn 'em.' Now Bren was sitting on the bed, holding herself steady against the swaying of the bus. Outside, it had gone quiet, the raid fading away as they went through the Blackwall Tunnel, north under the Thames. And Bren was holding the bunk frame with

one hand, holding the other out to take the kid back
– who was still screeching and clinging to Johnnie.

'What you want 'er for?'

'She's got to come to Mummy. '

'So's you can thump 'er?'

Bren shook her head. 'Take off them wet things.'

Johnnie didn't know what to do; the little girl was
clutching harder still round his neck, pulling herself
into him, like a monkey into its mother.

'Mummy!' she was wailing. 'Want my mummy!'

'Give her here.' Bren was going to get up and come
to grab her if she had to. A slight change in her voice.
'Your mummy's here, darlin'.'

Not sure, Johnnie took the girl towards her – as she
screeched louder, dug her nails into his neck, tried
with her pathetic little strength to force him back the
other way. For all that, he took her over to where Bren
was holding out her arms for her.

He spoke softly, like his dad on a threat. 'You clout
'er an' I'll knock your teeth out!'

'Get off!' Bren wiggled the girl's nose. 'Uncle
Johnnie's stupid, ain't he, baby? Mummy's not going
to smack, not for now.'

As gently as he could against the rock of the vehicle, Johnnie handed the fighting, screeching, hiccup-
ing girl to where Bren had spread her knees apart and
was waiting for her to be lain there.

'Smelly, eh? Erky-perky ponky!' Bren took no
notice of the red face and the shouting, held the girl
down with one hand and unbuttoned the rompers,
had them and the knickers off in one go. 'Wear a pair

of mine!' she said. 'Be like Mummy, eh?' Out from under her, Bren pulled a pair of pink drawers, big enough for two girls the size of the one across her lap.

Right now Johnnie didn't know whether to look or turn away. But he was supposed to be protecting the kid from another smack so he looked, and learned a bit. And being on show to the world, the little girl suddenly started a real kicking, and caught Bren with a toe in the eye – for which she got a great hard smack on her backside.

'Yaaowl!' She kicked again, delirious at this assault.

'Naughty little tyke! Mustn't kick Mummy!'

But Johnnie's mouth had filled up with the taste of violence and his heart was going. His hand was a fist and he was all for punching Bren smack in the face. Except the bus swerved a bit, Bren ducked to fight the pink drawers on, and the violent second had gone.

'Yaaaowl! Mu-u-um!' Hic. 'Mu-u-uum!'

'Leave 'er, can't you? You're scuddin' 'andy, ain't you?' Johnnie was ready to fight her for a hold of the kid.

'Got to be, with babies. But she's my baby an' I'm her mummy, so she knows.' And Bren pulled the girl up to her and rocked her hard against the trying to get away.

Which was interrupted by the hard rap of something metal on a window; and as Johnnie twisted round, there was the face of Tommy Price, bashing his ring on the driver's window and staring through.

'What the – !' he was mouthing. And Johnnie realized that the bus had stopped, and next thing that the face wasn't there. Pricey was coming round. Coming round for a sort-out. In a panic he looked about, but there wasn't any hiding place in here. And it was like the little girl knew, too, because as Johnnie leant over to open the door, she shut her crying and looked down the bus – scared stiff.

'Where the hell has *she* come from?' Pricey rocked the bus on its springs as he came in, with the look on him that he'd go straight on and through the opposite side. But he pushed down the gangway, left Johnnie to get out of his road and stood, angry, over Bren and the kid. 'What the God Almighty game is *this*?'

Shaking, the little kid tried to hide herself, all eyes and wide-open mouth; the face gone from red to milk white in one big drain.

'She's Bren's baby.'

To Johnnie, it was as if the man turned right round and got back facing her again -- all without moving. His long hair, streaky yellow, fell down over his face. His neck had puffed up like a knuckle-fighter's and his eyes had gone to pin-holes.

'Get her out of it!'

'Get lost!' Bren cuddled the terrified kid, who was clutching her now all right.

'We're over Walthamstow. They've packed up bombing. Give you a brainbox 'stead of a bowl o' porridge an' you'd hear the all-clear any minute.'

'Bren's baby's not going nowhere!'

'Whose game's this? This Old Nell's? She with you?' Tommy Price had rounded on Johnnie.

'Never seen her before.'

49

The man got hold of Bren's hair and shook her like a broken doll. 'Bren's *not* got a baby! Right? Now put her out!' He slapped his wife's head free with a backhander. 'Someone can pick her up an' take her back. We let her go when we get down the country, she'll get ate by wild dogs. You want that?'

Johnnie's stomach was nowhere it ought to be. The man frightened him anyway: he'd seen his sort over Aldgate, ruling the roost, drunk or sober – but this one had gone from one to the other so fast he was behaving the worst of both. He'd kill with those bare hard hands if it meant keeping the nosy police out of his way.

'Give her here!' And in one grab Tommy Price had the kid under his arm as if she were a dog off to get drowned.

'Don't you . . . !' As the kid went so Bren was up and climbing at Pricey's back, scratching at his neck, pulling his hair and getting the nails in. 'Give her back! Give her back!'

But to Pricey it seemed like no more than a mozzy. He shook her off, was at the door and opening it, halfway out to get shot of the kid. From behind him Johnnie could see a blaze from the docks, but right here it was dark and all alone, looked like a bit of a park or common.

Pricey couldn't put the kid out here: she'd die of fright, if nothing else.

And she was kicking and screaming, wailing for her mum. Johnnie had never had a mum; but he knew what his dad going off had been like.

'Oi! You! Put 'er down!'

Tommy Price was all for just slinging her out, you could see the way his back was going under his overcoat. But when he heard Johnnie he just stopped, one foot on a step, one on the ground outside. He didn't look round. For a second he was listening, and not believing, letting the kid have her kick and scream.

Johnnie stood his ground. The man couldn't swipe him from there, not without letting go.

'You put her out and I'm out an' all.'

'Oh, yeah, do me fine!' Now the man turned back, the kid still under his arm, like some farmer haggling on the way to slaughter.

'An' I'll finger you! Right? Dukes's gypsy site, I know where you're off to, you ain't got nowhere else to go with this old crock. So I'll tell 'em where you are, an' I'll tell 'em *who* you are.' Johnnie could hardly breathe, his chest had gone all tight on him. But he'd meant what he said; except Tommy Price could probably do for the two of them, if he wanted to take that chance.

'You got big pigging ears for a scrap of old horsemeat, ain't you?'

'I ain't stupid, if that's what you mean!'

'Mum! I want my mummy!' And another fit of screeching and kicking, which Tommy Price just shook quiet.

'Clever! So you goin' back yourself, are you? To your approved school? 'Cos that's what telling on me's gonna get you.' The man looked set now to do the putting out. And Johnnie had sewn himself right

51

up, because he'd made a threat, which Tommy Price couldn't ever forget.

'Ever 'eard o' *writing*? Ever 'eard of a police-box telephone? I don't 'ave to go in nowhere to tell on you. Just your name, and your regiment, and where you are.' The man was eyeing him really hard. But suddenly he came back into the bus and threw the kid back at Bren by the bed.

'Shut her up!' Pricey said. 'And you, son, *you* – you say every prayer you know while I get us to Dukes's, because when we get there you're gonna wish you was back in your villains' school a million times over!' He shut the door with a slam, came back to make it all moonlight clear. 'I'm gonna have the skin on you singing so loud they'll hear it over Germany!' And he slammed himself out with a shake that had the safest pot of all coming off its hook.

'Bren's baby!' the big girl crooned, rocking and hugging the kid, ignoring Johnnie. But the child was in hysterics now. She was coughing and spitting and screaming and then choking on a silence, before drawing breath to start all over.

By a miracle Bren didn't give up. She didn't push the kid off when she wouldn't stop, but instead she went on singing some wild song from out of her tuneless head and she rocked and rocked her baby – until after a long, tired, whining dribble the kid at last put her thumb in her mouth and went off. Not so much to sleep as unconscious.

Johnnie wrapped himself down under his coat again and tried to plan what he was going to do. Get out of that door when the bus next slowed down and work his way back to Plumstead? Or, better – and more likely, seeing as how Pricey wasn't slowing down for even the sharpest bends now – out quick when the bus stopped at Dukesey's and scram into the woods or trees or whatever was there. Then he could give the site the once-over. Because Dukesey's might be his best chance, when Pricey had calmed down, tucked away with the gippos till word came that they'd found his dad.

4

JOHNNIE didn't know what he'd find at the gypsy site – except that they wouldn't find him. Before Pricey could pull the handbrake on he'd be out of that bus like a winner down at Hackney dog racing. He'd be into the woods before those wheels stopped going round. In his head he saw the bus pulling up to a ring of caravans with a fire in the middle and a great pot stewing on it: men in wide hats and women in shawls, staring at him and not saying a dicky bird. Except they wouldn't be staring at him for long. All the journey, he kept looking at the bus door, saw its handle, seemed to feel it in his hand, kept going over how he'd grab it and slide it and go. Into the woods and through the other side and hide out in some barn till Tommy Price had gone off the boil and they'd sorted it all out about the kid. And then he'd come back and tell them who he was, and give them the ration book Old Nell had stuffed into his pocket.

They were a way out of London now, had to be, but it was a long old while before there was any sign of pulling up or slowing down. The little kid was sleeping and Bren had gone off as well, like some big girl cuddling her doll. He looked out a couple of times, but there were no clues and signs to tell him where they were going; except once, bashing on through a village, a shop said 'Little Amwell Post Office'. But where was that? It wasn't like saying 'Southend'.

But Southend or South Pole, for all his stewing and planning, when they got there he was wrong. Wrong about the place and wrong about what went off. Right in the middle of thinking about his ideal barn – with deep straw for the sleeping and eggs where the hens had laid them – the bus suddenly stopped, sharp as if a dog had run out, and around the front were a couple of loud men banging on Tommy Price's door.

'It's midden o' the night!' one of them shouted.

'What you want, who you after?' the other one took up. Dogs barked, one and then another trying to cap it.

By then, Johnnie was over at the side door in that quick flash he'd planned, trying to slide it open – except that already there was a hard grip on the other side, and no chance in the world of moving it.

'Hold your rush!' someone else shouted. 'What's your business?' Another loud bark, choked, like something being held off at the throat.

Johnnie let go. Pricey wouldn't be knocking any seven bells out of him, not yet anyhow, because he wasn't going to be top dog. From the sounds of it he was going to have to watch his step with these blokes.

The door opened. Pricey was led round by the two men and brought back into the bus. They were older men like Grandad Stubbs, dressed the way he did, with flat caps and jackets, one of them with a crossed scarf over a shirt without a collar. And there was another man, with long smoky-grey hair hanging down to his neck and a knitted jumper zipped up to his chin. He came in first and half closed his eyes, looking down the bus to where the bed was, with Bren starting to sit herself up.

'Brenda . . .? That you there, Brenda Lee?'

'Uncle Dukesey . . .' She sat up, pulled up the top rug on the bunk, hid the kid, who was asleep.

The others looked at Johnnie, and then up and down, took everything in.

'Got yourself a van, then?' Dukesey was asking. 'Motor?'

'That's about it.' Tommy Price was shrugging himself straight in his big coat, trying to get himself back on level pegging.

The gypsy didn't look at Tommy Price. 'You're the geyro she married.'

'Same one.'

'So what's this bum's rush for, getting the dogs a'going?' He tossed his head at the door as a horse somewhere near gave a whinny. Now he did turn and look at Tommy Price, and Johnnie could see how you wouldn't argue with Dukesey, not even with him being old. 'Heard you coming from the bottom of Barrows Lane.'

Somewhere outside a kid shouted in its sleep, and then went quiet again. A dog growled, like waiting for an answer.

'Bad raid. Bren got scared. Old Nell Stubbs told us to get out of it 'fore she started –' He nodded his head at Bren, but he said no more, as if he was not too certain whether they thought she was barmy, too. 'She don't like the raids.'

56

'Who do?'

Dukesey went on looking round the bus, but the others eased off, started backing out of the door. All the same, Johnnie knew there were two big bits of business to be done, only waiting their time. And one of them was him.

'And who are you, boy?' The gippo had to have a mind that could see inside you. Johnnie had eyed the door, and by the misty light coming up he'd seen what was outside of it – a bit of hedge and then a wide and heavy ploughed field like a big grey sea. He wasn't running off into any woods, sure as eggs.

'Johnnie Stubbs. Old Nell said give you this.' He pulled the scruffy ration book out of his back pocket.

Dukesey took it but didn't look at it, shoved it in his jumper. 'Which one of the Stubbses?' He hadn't stopped staring, and he wasn't a man you gave a smart-arse answer to, once you were a bit of his business.

'Old Nell lives with Wally. 'E's my grandad. 'Is boy's Arthur, gone in the army. My dad. We lost the run of 'im.' The old man was still looking at Johnnie hard. 'Got the second-hand shop up Brick Lane.'

Now Dukesey turned to the two men outside. 'Nelly Quinn, went settled. Looks to Brenda.'

The nearer one of them squinted at the sun coming up. 'Yeah. Well, I'm for checking the traps.'

'Given we're up.' The other didn't sound over the rainbow with Dukesey Joyce having relatives like Pricey and Johnnie and Bren.

Dukesey pinned Tommy Price with those eyes.

'There's three outfits here. Them two and me. Rub along misto, an' that's the way it's liked. No fights.' He poked his head out of the door, squinting at the lie of the land. 'Fetch this van along through to the far end, by me. Not now, we won't wake the camp for the sake of an hour.'

Somewhere out there a horse blew through its nostrils. And Johnnie felt more sure than ever that Tommy Price wouldn't lay a finger on him now. Things wouldn't be misto for long if he did.

'You lying low?' Dukesey suddenly asked. Johnnie jumped, but the old man was still eyeing Pricey.

'Could say that . . .'

'*Could* say? I'm asking straight.'

Johnnie looked at Pricey, found it hard not to grin: Dukesey Joyce wasn't going to be messed around.

The deserter nodded. 'I'll keep out the way.'

'Well, my boy's gone.' Dukesey threw a hand over a shoulder, meaning – like Johnnie's dad – who knew where? 'He can't write, I can't read, so we'll see him one day. Others, the Stokeses and the Boswells –' he jerked his head towards the world the other side of the furthest hill – 'one's gone back to Ireland and the other's headed for Dorset.'

'Told you, I won't show myself.'

'Outside of working the scrap with us. You ain't living for free.'

Dukesey pulled the ration book out of his jumper, riffled through it to see what coupons were left. It was full. He looked at the front cover. 'This don't say "Stubbs", do it?' He had turned it to Johnnie.

Johnnie read it. He wasn't a bad reader, wrote out some of his dad's receipt books, checked the odd bill; had once started *Treasure Island*, but got the hump with it. This writing was harder, tall and thin, as if the book belonged to a lady like old Queen Mary. *Surname: Freeman. Other names: Emma Sarah.* There was a Plumstead address. He made it out, and told Dukesey.

'Know her?'

Johnnie shook his head.

'Got herself under a bomb,' Tommy Price interrupted. 'Likely. Her old man's sold it for a few bob.'

Dukesey shoved it back into his pocket. 'We boil up the one skillet on the fire, bake three or four tins of bread, but you find your own share of the food.'

'I can feed three mouths.'

Johnnie's head ricked round, couldn't stop a look down the bus at the bed. *Three* mouths? So what did that mean Pricey was going to do about the kid? There were four with her. Was he going to dump her, *kill* her like he said? Or was he just keeping her secret from Dukesey?

But Dukesey had been streets ahead of him all through. He was pointing a fag-stained finger at Bren. 'What you got wriggling under there? You hiding a dog, girl? 'Cos if it goes country mad –' He turned back to Tommy Price, while Bren got out of bed, smiling like a kid at Christmas. Showing him the sleepy kid.

'She's Bren's baby . . .' the big girl said.

'You jumped the broomstick on account o' this?'

Dukesey looked angry, like he'd been fooled when he gave the nod to the wedding.

'No way. Not ours. She's a waif an' stray.' Tommy Price had lost so much of his edge, he looked like a man caught between the Flying Scotsman and a set of Euston buffers.

'You evacuatin' her?'

'That's about it.'

'Bren's baby.'

But now the kid was coming to and taking this in. She was waking up to it all: a dark, cold bus, a wet bed, a big loud man with hair hanging down around his shoulders, that bully in the doorway, and this big girl who'd given her a thumping in the night.

'Evacuation, eh?' Dukesey pushed back to the door of the bus, grunted for a laugh as he went. 'Makes sense of being Romany, don't it?'

Which were the last clear words anyone was going to hear. Suddenly the kid started screaming and kicking and fighting to get to the door, shouting for her mum and her dad. And the only answer Bren and Pricey had was his hand over her mouth and her having a hard try to smack the kid into shutting up.

But Johnnie wasn't having that, no more than he was last night. He got himself between the pair of them and the girl again, and he held her tight, and cuddled her, and talked the biggest load of rubbish in her ears – this side then that as she twisted and squirmed like a creature who didn't know the words *give in*.

'All right, darling, all right, doll. Yeah, yeah. We'll

find Mummy, eh? Johnnie will. And your dad. They won't be long, will they?' he asked the others. '*Will they?*'

'Don' ask me.' Pricey was sucking a bitten finger.

'*I'm* her mum. Mummy's here!' Bren tried to land another smack. 'Shut your face, will you, you little cow?'

But the kid had woken the camp. Children's voices could be heard somewhere outside, irritable, and a woman shouted to keep the noise down, for Our Lady's sake. The sound of someone chopping could just be heard above the screeching, and as Tommy Price took down the black-out the light of morning came in cold.

'An' I'm shifting this bus,' Pricey said, going for the door. 'Then you can leave her to scream an' get the stove going, right?' He cuffed Johnnie round the head. 'An' if we're stuck with her,' he shouted above another wave, 'tell her she'll get used to us or she won't sit down for a twelve-month, right?' And he went to rev the engine.

Johnnie kept cuddling the little one – until in the middle of another shout and struggle she suddenly shook, differently, violently, head to toe, and as if a spell had been waved above her, she stopped her fight; and through the bubbling wet of her eyes and nose she stood still and stared through Johnnie.

'All right,' he said. 'Good girl, good girl.' He kissed her in the hair, waiting for the start-up again.

But she didn't. She went on staring through him. 'Pip, Squeak an' Wilfred,' she said. 'Pip, Squeak an'

Wilfred. Shirley wants Pip, Squeak an' Wilfred.' All in a faint, baby voice.

The names from the comic strip he knew. But – 'That *your* name?' he asked her, quietly. 'You called Shirley?'

'Pip, Squeak an' Wilfred,' was all she would say, as if it weren't her saying it, not the gutsy kid who'd been fighting and shouting, but some wheedling little baby, gone back years.

Johnnie looked up at Bren, who was pulling on her slacks and steadying herself as the bus started bumping across a verge of some sort.

'Hear what she said?' he asked her. 'Says 'er name's Shirley.'

'No, it ain't!' Bren snapped. 'She's my baby. An' she's what I call her.'

'But she's got a name. She's Shirley Someone.'

'My Pip, Squeak an' Wilfred,' Shirley was going on, like a mechanical doll.

'You get dressed and you play with Mummy!' Bren shouted at her, down the bus. 'See?' She rubbed a dry flannel round her own face. 'And you ain't called Shirley, that's a stupid name. You're gonna be Kathleen. Little Kath, an' nothing else. You got it?'

But Shirley was looking at Johnnie Stubbs as if she hadn't heard. 'Pip, Squeak an' Wilfred,' she said, in that same baby voice.

Vera Lewis was lying still in her hospital bed. It would have been hard to tell the difference between life and death except Reg was holding her hand under the covers, and the hand was warm. And there was the slightest, most fragile sound of breathing, and now and then a startling sort of snore. It was the Monday morning and Reg was off duty, out of uniform and given forty-eight hours' compassionate leave.

He looked empty: his eyes were hollow and his cheeks were drained. His hands were cooler than Vera's where blood had gone from the surface in the body's defence against attack. And he *had* been attacked. His wife was teetering on the edge of death and his daughter was nowhere, blown to kingdom come by German high explosive, with not even a shoe to hold in his hand and kiss.

The sister of the night before marched past, somehow still as crackling with medical energy as if she'd just come out of the Nurses' Home after a good night's sleep. 'Chin up!' she commanded Reg. 'Keep talking to her!'

Reg did as he was told; at least, he pulled himself up in the chair and leant over Vera's peaceful face. But that was as far as it went. What could he say, what words could he use to make her want to come back to him? And, anyhow, was it fair to bring her to life with Shirley gone for ever? Honest to God, wasn't Vera better off where she was? There wasn't ever going to be any 'happy ever after' for him or for her; so wasn't sliding away into death what he ought to want?

Except he had his needs, too; and could he bear to lose both his girls?

No, he couldn't. That would be too much. He blew

his nose, to cover up wiping his eyes, and he gently leant forward and started calling Vera's name, as if all he wanted was for her to come and see something little Shirley was up to.

Dukesey's site was no more than a lay-by off a country road, at the point where it widened before a bend. It was on highish ground and there was natural shelter where the verge between the lay-by and the road rose and took the wind up and over the vans. It was nicely out of the way of the towns and not on any farmer's land, and the women and children were being useful with the potato picking. So no one moved them on.

There was an old open lorry at one end of the site, and then the three bow-top wagons which the Stokeses, the Boswells, and the Dukesey Joyces lived in. And up beyond – on a bit of a tilt – was the spot where Tommy Price had been told to pull over.

There was nothing of the fancy gypsy encampment in this long strung-out site. The fire, when it was lit, was small and scrappy, just a few sticks. And instead of being slung over a spit, the pot itself was bedded askew among the wood and ashes, alongside a big tin kettle. All along the hedgerow was the washing, hung out to dry among the leaves, and there was no grass underfoot, just mud. What did give the place the feel of the films were those three gypsy caravans parked up alongside the hedge: maroon wagons with tops which came out like well-baked loaves from narrow tins, and steps up to half-and-half doors, and painted decorations down the woodwork and on the spokes of the wheels. And then there were the tents, two of them, where from the sound of it some of the children slept, tarpaulin jobs they called benders, low and bowed over and circular, their coverings fixed to a wooden framework through scorched holes.

And it was out of the benders that trouble came. Trouble in the way Johnnie was used to, plus trouble in a new way.

As the sun rose higher and Monday morning took hold, the women – who Johnnie was going to take a while to sort, because the older and the younger didn't look so different in the outdoor life – these mothers and grans got going with a fire and started cooking breakfast. And as bacon and scrambled eggs and fried cabbage came off the fire, and fresh baked bread came out of a tin, and as Johnnie's stomach started telling him he hadn't eaten since before the war, out came the kids from the tents.

As soon as the younger ones started rolling out and they saw the bus, they ran off to look at it as if it were some new invention. They kicked at the tyres and put their hands to warm on the engine grille. But when they'd done with inspecting the bus, they started inspecting Johnnie.

Which was OK for the younger kids, the ones of Johnnie's age and down. The one he worried about first, and the most, was the biggest, a kid older than him they called Christy as if he was Jesus Christy – who had a mouth like it always had a cigarette dangling from it, although it didn't. And he had those dark eyes giving the message that they didn't blink too much at anything. This one didn't come out of his tent yawning and pushing up at the trees and scratching like the others. He came out ready set for a hard day, and Johnnie never saw him any different. He was one of those people who look the same every waking moment: same clothes, same twist of the mouth, same walk. While his little brother and sister went to find their mother in the van, he came over to where Johnnie was stood by the fire with a mug in his hand, and he just took the mug, and he threw out the tea, and he filled it from the kettle without bothering with the rag holder. And he walked off behind the hedge to where some sort of canvas arrangement poked into a field of something growing.

Johnnie did nothing, watched him go. *HMS Greengates* had taught him a lot about giving in when giving in was best. Now that he was miles from Aldgate, all he wanted was a quiet tuck-in somewhere. Time to think, work things out. Hang quiet if he wanted till his dad came marching home. So he crouched himself down like a good underdog, made himself small.

And then came the girl. She was about his own age and the women called her Biddy. From the first look she seemed to see the inside of him. And she stood and eyed, and gave him what could have been a smile – he wasn't sure – but enough of something to have him pretending to poke at the fire with a smouldering stick. And he didn't know why, but she'd put spit into his mouth, and had him with a hand to the grass to stop himself going over unbalanced.

She had brown eyes, and long, straggly, shiny hair, and she was in a woolly jumper and a long tartan skirt, and black boots with furry flaps folded down outside.

'Got a name?' she asked him. Only it was like an invitation to dance.

He wanted to say yes and let her take the bones out of that, the way he bossed Woodseer Street and Brick Lane. But he told her. 'Johnnie.'

'Johnnie what?'

'Stubbs.'

She had a hand on her hip. 'Stubbs? Like fag ends?'

'Sort of.'

'Your van?' She didn't look round at the bus, just fluttered her fingers at what was behind her. He'd given the quickest of looks up, and he nodded.

'Can't see your face.'

Obediently, instantly, he looked up again.

'Kushti, aren't you?' she said.

'Eh?'

'Pretty.'

And she'd turned to the fire and started dishing out breakfast to the younger kids who were crowding round: porridge first, then a gritty plate of the fry-up for Johnnie, handed to him without a word or another look.

Pretty? Pretty *tough*, he'd say. But he knew he'd gone hot. It wasn't this titchy fire, either. He started to eat, with the fork he'd been thrown – which had to be Christy's moment to come back from the other side of the hedge, and to stand there as if he were making up his mind whether or not to have Johnnie's plate to go with his cup. But he didn't; which could have been him reading the look on Johnnie's face that said he'd butt him in the stomach and have him in the fire if he tried that on.

As it happened, Tommy Price came out of the bus just then and started making a great fuss of the fire, puffing at it as if he knew what he was up to, putting on more wood and only making more smoke. One of the old women quickly pushed a couple of plates into his hand to see him off back to the Leyland.

'And porridge for the girlie,' she said, dolloping on a third. Which Pricey took as well, doing a balancing act, backing off.

'An' who's he?' Christy wanted to know – but really meaning who was Johnnie?

Johnnie wiped the last smear of egg with the rest of the bread.

'I said, "Who's he?"' Christy was standing over him, all boot.

'Ask him.'

The boot lifted.

But the brown-eyed girl they called Biddy had come up on the other side of Johnnie with a bucket for his dirty plate. 'In there,' she said. 'You're along o' the juvels.' Johnnie took his eye off the boot, looked up at her, didn't understand. 'Clean the tins, then you're going to lift spuds down the back.'

Johnnie frowned.

'We all gotta work, son.' Christy's lips never moved a lot. 'An' you're along of the women.' He started helping himself to a big breakfast, the second lot to go on as the older men came towards the fire. 'Women an' kids.'

'Come on.' Biddy had hold of Johnnie's arm, was pulling him up. 'You want over the bor?' She was nodding her head at the hedge.

Johnnie thought. He wanted a pee, but no more. 'I'll find my way for a quick one.'

'Mind the beck. Go downside, we get the drinking from the other.'

He went for the hedge, was about to duck under a line of washing on thick string, between a tree and a driven post: a skirt and embroidered blouses.

'No! Stop!' Biddy was coming to him, a teacher look on her face. 'Men don't go under women's wear. It's unclean.'

'Oh.' It all looked clean enough to him. But you didn't upset people more than you had to. He went well round the line of washing and found the gap in the hedge Christy had used. A decent sun was coming up but it was still colder away from the fire. He rubbed his hands and wished he had more warm clothes, but he'd run from the approved school on a warm night, and there hadn't been any going back for a jumper.

He stepped on to the edge of the crop, whatever it was. Now he was through on the other side, he could see why the camp was set up where it was. Trickling along the side of the field, tucked under the hedge like a secret, was a small stream, no more than an inch deep. It followed the fall of the land, moved slowly and made no noise. And it didn't take a lot of common sense to know how useful that was; because aside from the clean water for drinking and cooking, here was a natural little lavatory, as well as being a pull to the creatures these gypsies caught for food.

He looked around to check he was private, then fished himself out. He could guess what a crime it was if you did any of this on the upside of the camp. And he peed, a strong golden arc that he watched as it steamed, sort of felt a friendship for, at least being something of his: a drop which had been with him since the air raid the night before, tucked under the shelter with Old Nell.

And he was in the middle of that soft thought when he was suddenly pushed in the middle of the back. Sneaked up on, shoved into the hedge face-first, feet freezing in the cold of the stream, and him finishing his pee down the inside of his trousers.

He twisted round, ready for the next attack. His hand went to himself where he might be kicked. But Christy was doing no more than walking away from him, not looking round, inviting an attack from behind – but ready for it, sure as eggs. No doubt with a knife handy.

Johnnie swore, but not out loud. He pulled himself out of the water, sorted himself – wet and cold outside, wet and warm in – and decided he wouldn't do anything stupid. *Bide your time*, his dad would say.

He'd wait. What he couldn't stop was the standing and swearing while his heart went mad and anger seared inside him like a poker stuck into a spud. And he was so rigid with his own rage that he didn't even hear the sudden loud screeching coming from the bus – as little Shirley had the salty porridge forced down inside her by her new, spiteful mother.

Monday. The first day of another new life.

5

JOHNNIE STUBBS was used to hard work – weekends and holidays and days off school when his dad was pushed – but his back had never felt broken like it did right now. Lifting potatoes was hard, solid graft. They'd gone out from the site with the dew still wet on the grass, riding on what they called the lorry – an open, tilted cart, pulled by one of the horses. And he'd just about got used to keeping his balance without hanging on to the nearest kid all the time, when they were there. At the edge of a big field which seemed to reach to Russia, going by its size and the cold coming off it. There was him, and the girl Biddy, and a couple of other boys and girls a bit younger, and five women, old and not so old, wrapped in their scarves and shawls and going on about various things. Like, Grandpa Stokes feeling the ramble on him but having to stay in the camp on account of the potato picking; Granny Joyce out calling, selling firewood instead of pegs while the war was on; how the men weren't getting rabbits with much meat on; and other stuff with words he didn't understand.

When he first saw the field he thought the long lines across it had been ploughed with the aid of a ruler. They were straight as a parting in Brylcreem hair, ritzy to look at, but when you had to work your way along them bent double, you didn't think they were so smart. On top of which, the ground was as cold as the cemetery and the spuds were like balls of ice.

Johnnie moved on down the line, lifting the bare potatoes and throwing them into the basket they pulled with them. The boy forking the furrow was going fast, not leaving much unturned. It was gruelling just keeping up.

'Farmer pay all right?' It might take the edge off if there was something at the end of all this grief.

'Dunno how much.' Biddy was working the next furrow, spud for spud about level. 'Gets given to Granny Joyce. She holds the purse.'

He knew women who liked to do that. Auntie Pearl, his dad's girlfriend, for a start.

'We get a few coppers pocket money, but she don't drop it in too heavy.' Biddy stopped in her stoop, looked across at him a bit saucy. 'Enough to buy yourself a bright little diklo.'

'Eh? Buy what?'

'Proper scarf for your throat.'

'What'd I want with one of them? Pair o' mitts, me.' He rubbed his cold hands together.

'Oh, they're special.' One of the other girls giggled, and they got on a few more yards towards the end of the furrow. Johnnie worked on to reach the end, but if he thought the getting there was going to give him a tea break he was wrong – because it was a step along the hedge and straight back down in the other direction. Still, hard graft though it was, once you got into

73

it there was a sort of peace about it. It could have been there wasn't a war on at all. Down at *HMS Greengates* he'd been near a bomber base, and he'd hear them roaring off at night, and back in the morning. But there was nothing here, you could even hear a bird singing, slung up high over the next field. There was smoke coming from a few fields away, which in London would have meant some disaster; but it was only the burning of the stubble, no sweat to anything but the fieldmice.

A couple of hours like that – bending, scooping, throwing spuds and dragging the basket, emptying it into the sacks every time it was full – and there *was* a quick stop for a drop of tea. There wasn't any shout, but by some secret sign everyone stopped and went to the sheltered end of one of the furrows where the old woman Boswell had got a bit of fire going and a kettle on. And there were just enough tin mugs to include Johnnie. But he'd only just begun easing his muscles when Biddy started something buzzing.

'That little kid kicked up a shindig in the night.' She was sitting on a mat with her legs straight out, relaxed, but proper.

'Bellyache, or suthink . . .'

'Scared, more like. Like she'd seen a mulo.'

Johnnie shrugged, drank his hot tea. He didn't know what a mulo was but he guessed it was some sort of ghost. He let it ride. He had his own item to talk about.

'Drank the full cup this time!'

'Christy? He's gone with the men,' she said. She knew. 'Logging, a bit of scrap.'

'Good job.' Johnnie made to get up to go for a pee down in the far copse.

'That always happens.'

'Oh, yeah?'

'"Cock of the camp". There's always one out of the men an' one out of the boys.'

'Well, 'e can be it for me. Only 'ad to ask.'

'An' he is.' She looked into her mug, at the tea-leaves in the bottom before she threw them out. 'Every school we go to, the boys have to fight.'

'Same 'ere.'

'An' if you go on a big site, there's always one man who's the cock.'

'Dukesey Joyce?'

'He is here.' The women weren't watching and she stopped sitting so straight, leant in to him a bit, pulled her feet up under her skirt. The shift had him looking at her eyes – big, and bright, and a flecky sort of greeny brown – the sort of eyes you couldn't look away from, not fixed on you like that. 'There's a camp we go to the other side of Romford. In the middle of it there's a big heap of dirt, and when you pull on with your wagons there's a mush called Liney Silks who jumps up on top of the heap and flaps his arms like a fighting bantie, and he cock-a-doodle-do's, and if anyone fancies being cock of the camp they have to go and do the same, and then they fight.'

'Anyone done it?'

Now she sat back away from him, her head up,

looked at him proudly, and came forward to be confidential again, her sweet breath in his face. 'My dad did. Wisdom Boswell. And he half killed Liney Silks – because that's what you have to do, it's to the death if it has to be – and he was cock while we was there.'

'Good on 'im!' Well, he'd have felt that swell about his dad, except he was a smaller type of bloke altogether, more your wheeler and dealer.

'But Liney Silks is still there, cocking it.'

''Ow come?'

'Because we're not.'

'An' which one's your dad?' Johnnie asked, because he'd want to know who to give that respect to.

'He died of something inside him.'

'Ah.' Now Johnnie was going for a pee. And the others were breaking up, setting themselves for the next stretch of potato picking.

But Biddy was offering her hand to be pulled up. He took it, and brought her to her feet. And her fingers and palm were warm from being round her mug, and there was a sudden tingle where he'd never had one before, and he had to hurry to the trees in case it meant he was going to wet himself.

Biddy had the last word, though. As she stamped her feet into her boots for comfort, she caught him with a flyer. 'That kid, in your bus,' she said. 'She don't cry kushti, do she?'

So who was that little girl who reckoned her name was Shirley? As Johnnie wet the leaves of a bush, he knew he couldn't go on forever pushing her out of his head. He'd stood up to Tommy Price to stop her getting dropped out of the bus, but he hadn't dared to start wondering what the hell she was doing there, anyhow.

Had Bren stolen her off someone? Because she had gypsy blood in her, did Bren, and didn't they say gypsies ran off with people's babies? From the start at his grandad's yard all he'd ever heard her going on about was her babies, those stupid little dolls: loony all right, but loony people did loony things. And the kid was in her sleeping clothes, she hadn't been dressed for going out walking. So, what? Had Bren slipped off after Pricey had gone over the pub and got in a window? Had the kid been all asleep tucked up, and Bren come in through her bedroom window and lifted her? Didn't have to be from the rows of proper houses. Back of the yard across the fields there were loads of little bungalows. Bren wouldn't have needed a ladder for getting into one of them, would she?

He shook himself at the bush and got sorted – while someone shouted at him from over in the field to get himself back, quick.

The rest of the morning got no better for his back. He'd feel this for ever, he reckoned, turn into a little humpy man like Newspaper Arnold over Aldgate if he kept this up for more than a day at a time. But he'd always been a fighter, Johnnie Stubbs, he was known for it. So he didn't give in easy. If these gypsy kids could pick potatoes without calling a stop every five minutes, so could he.

'That a full Romany name, Stubbs?' Biddy asked him, out of nowhere, bent double. Then she squinted an eye at him. 'Your dad ever chor a kanny, or your mother dukker?'

'Yeah, all the time, but the wheels bust.' He knew what she was up to, she was talking her lingo at him, seeing if he knew it. From time to time they had gypsy kids at school in Wicks Street and they'd do their lingo in the playground like that, and get hit by the teachers for being secret.

'No, you ain't Romany, you ain't got the outside on your face.'

Which was a smacker, because Johnnie couldn't think of anyone less indoor than him. There hadn't used to be a night when his dad wouldn't have to shout him in from his street-raking and his penny-up-the-brewery-wall. But he wasn't going into all that, he was getting on with his lifting.

Except Biddy wasn't leaving it there. 'You ain't their boy, are you? Them two in the bus? They ain't old enough – well, she ain't.'

He took time to empty his basket, although it wasn't more than three parts full. 'Cousin. Evacuated with 'em.' And, thank God, it was left like that.

They had a break for a meal a bit later on, this time down in the copse. They'd taken the tea can from the other place and brewed up again, but this time with eggs to boil inside it, and they had them hard in the hand, with hunks of the heavy bread again and a couple of slices of cheese. Johnnie could have eaten a dray horse, and was surprised to see the younger boys having next to nothing before they went off for a game. But what he had filled him, and taking his ease like his dad did, he undid his belt button and sat himself against a tree where he could catch a bit of the sun from off the field.

But he couldn't catch a nap; kept his eyes closed to keep the others away, that was all.

Everything got more up in the air every day. What he was after kept changing. Right now he was out of the way a treat with these gypsies. No one from the Education around here was going to line him up with *HMS Greengates*, even if he *was* stopped. His hair grown long, his face turning gypsy in the country air, no one was going to match him with any picture they had. Except there was Christy. There was always a blessed Christy. Johnnie could smell trouble like Billingsgate fish, a mile off, and a quick pain came into his stomach as he lay there in the sun – a pain which said there was going to be a fight with that one long before the war was over. Sure as eggs.

And where was he going to sleep tonight? That was a nag. Last night hadn't counted, being on the move, but tonight – was he going to be down in a corner of the bus on the floor, with Pricey and Bren in the bunks, and the kid in there as well? Or where? In one of those tents with the boys – and cock of the camp Christy in there as well? He'd had all that in the approved school. They could do more things to you in a bed than anywhere else – have you waking up out of a nightmare to find it wasn't any nightmare at all.

He put a hand behind his neck, tried to look relaxed. So, what had he expected when he'd run from *HMS Greengates*? A soft touch? Heaven on earth? Just getting out, anywhere, that had been first – getting his stripy stinging bum out of the way of any more canes. It was only on the road that he'd made up his mind where he was going – back home to Woodseer Street to see what he could find for himself, to put him in the clear. Could be, move in with Auntie Pearl, if she'd hide him. But on the way he'd thought it out a bit. Round his way was the first place they'd look, into the empty house to see if he was camping there, or in the back room of his dad's old shop. And then they'd ask around, and someone – there'd got to be someone – would put the finger on him, even if they didn't mean to.

No, he hadn't headed straight for home; and when he smelt the sea coming off the river, the old family over Plumstead had come into his head as a good idea. Them on the other side of the water. Not that his dad ever talked about them much. They'd gone off their own ways a long while back. But, like he'd found, they *were* family. And it hadn't been too bad with Old Nell, till last night.

So now what? Well, it could have been the sun cheering him up, but this wasn't too bad, either. All he had to do was give best to Christy the cock as soon as he could, roll over in the fight like a loser and everything in the garden would be lovely.

'You want me to dukker you?'

That sat him up. Biddy had come over, and to be honest, he had heard the move of her skirt, but he'd hoped it was going on past.

'Give us your hand.' She took it anyway, on the left, and sat down by him, her legs straight and her boots touching again. And now he understood, as she smoothed his palm with her fingers and she felt the various bumps on it and traced the lines across. Dukkering was telling fortunes.

'You have to want it done.' She looked at him closely with those eyes and his mouth filled up with spit again. And did he want the dukkering done! Anything to keep her stroking his hand like that. It was like having his haircut off the daughter when the barber had gone in the navy. All the kids asked for a bit more off, just to keep it going, and came out of the shop like scalped cowboys.

'If you like.' And for all the wet in his mouth, his voice was as dry and croaky as a frog out of water.

They were on their own, the kids were off playing some horsy game in the trees, and the women were laughing at something round the other side by the fire.

But Biddy had taken a look and suddenly folded his hand shut. 'No,' she said, 'there ain't the time.'

'Get on. Don' believe in it, anyhow.' Because it wasn't on account of having no time, he knew that. What it was, she'd seen something she didn't like to tell him about. She'd shut him up like a Bible at a graveside. He spread his hand again, looked at it himself. 'One's for love, i'n't it? An' one's for life. Am I goin' to be bombed in a raid an' die?'

'No!'

'Well, what?'

'Told you, there's not the time.'

She was getting up; but he twisted, and pushed her shoulder down, a bit rough. 'You started it!' he said. 'I never asked. Now you carry on, all right? There ain't nothing you're goin' to scare me with!'

Biddy sat back, looked at him, big angry eyes which said she wasn't used to being pushed about. She was either going to shout and get up again, or do what he told her.

'All right. Come here.' She concentrated on his hand and wouldn't look in his eyes. It was as if she were really thinking out the words to say, under the cover of looking. He didn't care. It was all a load of mumbo-jumbo, anyhow.

'You ever been ill, big ill?' she asked.

He thought about it. 'I've been hurt,' he said. 'Been in big pain. But not your hospital sort.'

'Well, it's on here,' she said, tracing a finger from the side of his hand down to his wrist. 'Some great torment.' And then she took his other hand, his right, and she looked even harder at that. 'This is *you*,' she said, 'what you do. This –' and she tapped his left – 'this is what's foretold. But this don't have to be this.' Left, and then the right again. 'You can always do something about it.'

Johnnie was quick in the head, if nothing else. He understood. 'So this *great torment*, what you call it – is that on the other palm an' all?'

Now she looked him in the eye. 'Not yet,' she said.

Then it wasn't *HMS Greengates*. The torment was still on its way. But what a load of old rubbish! Except she was still running her finger over his hand.

'What about love? 'Ow'm I doing for that?'

'You ain't even got a scarf yet.'

'A scarf?'

'A diklo.'

'What's that got to do with love?'

'It's what you give the girl you're goin' to marry. Then she wears it, proud, an' no one else bothers her . . .'

'Ah.' He couldn't stop his eyes going to Biddy's neck. It was bare.

'Come on, then.' He pushed his hand up under hers.

She looked at his thumb, and gave it a little stroke. She smiled and opened her eyes wide at him. But instead of telling him what she'd seen on his love line, she put her forefinger to the tip of her nose. 'That's for me to know an' you to find out!'

And now she did get up, and did walk away, turning just the once, with a sway of the hip, looking over her shoulder at him before she went off round the trees to get back to the women.

Johnnie sat and looked at both his hands. But they were like two pages of a book with foreign words on them; he couldn't read that sort of stuff.

They stayed working the field until late, but not too

late. Johnnie had never had a watch, had never had much need for the exact time; they weren't wireless-listening people, him and his dad. But he thought it had to be about five o'clock when they packed up, and the younger boys got the horse back between the shafts and they dropped off the potato sacks in the farmer's yard.

Habit again, on the cart Johnnie kept himself turned away from anyone looking. He also yawned a lot, that changed the look of your face, and he blew his nose on his bit of rag, because people look away when you're sorting your nose out: those were tricks his dad knew. But no sweat, no one seemed to take much notice of him. He and the boys humped the sacks of potatoes into a barn filled with new hay, and, like it was their due, they collected a couple of sacks of that on their way out. And they were soon on the road again, and clopping at a steady pace back to the site, with Johnnie all no-hands this time. He was getting used to the life.

On the site he left the rest and made straight for the bus. The fire was going already and a brew-up was on, while one of the older women – and he reckoned this had to be Granny Joyce – was putting dough in tins into some sort of a metal oven. But if the fire was the main place for the others, the bus was where he belonged right now. Except he was cut off by Dukesey Joyce, working at something alongside it, by the side of the hedge.

'Here, boy,' he said.

Johnnie looked. There was a small tent, tucked in

neat, which hadn't been there that morning. It was like the others, only not so big: roughly circular and not very tall.

'You sleep here.' There wasn't any *if* or *but* about it, it was orders. Dukesey lifted the flap to show Johnnie the inside.

It was dark, and it smelt of the tarpaulin, but he could just make out the bendy rods that held the thing up, and a couple of mats pressing down the grass. And there were two or three horse blankets in there, piled as neat as inspection at *HMS Greengates*.

'They get fresh hay off Mr Jackson?' Dukesey asked.

Johnnie nodded.

'Then grab some of that for your bedding. An' change it regular.' And the old man had gone.

Johnnie didn't know whether he should say thank-you to be polite or leave it; so he left it. But he wasn't supposed to spend his life sitting in here, was he? If he had a home patch it was in the bus, with the kid. He came out of the tent. By the lack of the motor lorry, the men weren't back yet – which meant Pricey wasn't about – so he went to the bus and opened the door.

Bren was sitting on a chair the way she always did back at the yard, rocking a bit and singing something no one could ever make out. And Shirley, the little girl, was squatting near the door in a puddle of her own wee, tied round the neck like one of the horses to the leg of Bren's bunk. Saying nothing, staring at the open door as if she couldn't see.

'Jesus Christ!' said Johnnie, coming in, going out, coming in again.

'Pip, Squeak and Wilfred,' said Shirley in a voice which wasn't her own. And Johnnie's mouth started filling up with the taste of blood.

6

THE ROPE across Flaxton Road had been taken down, and the way was open again to traffic. Shirley's house and most of the place next door were just another roped-off bomb site, waiting to be made safe. A policeman or the Civil Defence came by now and then to stop any kids playing on the mound of old bricks, but it was only for their own safety.

Reg Lewis, on the last of his compassionate leave, had left Vera in the hospital and was searching like a scavenger through the debris of his house. People did that after raids, but usually quicker than this, looking for hoarded tins of food, or money, or someone else's useful bits and pieces; lumps of coal, even. But Reg Lewis wasn't about anything like that. This had been his house; and if anyone had tried to take him away from his own old home he would have given them as hard a fight as any cock of the heap.

Something, anything of his little girl was what he wanted. A shoe, a sock, a page from a favourite book. You had to have something to hold, to cry over, something to keep in a drawer till you died yourself. He lifted bricks and bits of masonry, he kicked earth and shifted a broken banister he had grained and varnished in the spring. And he peeled aside stiff rips of kitchen lino, patterns Shirley had hopscotched on, now just so much debris. But he couldn't find a button or a bow of the girl, not a toy or a doll or a stitch of her clothes; just a torn half-page of her old annual blowing about, that's all there was, so he shoved it into his pocket.

He stood on top of the heap and looked around him. The whole neighbourhood was different now, with the space opened up by the bomb. He could see the backs of houses he'd never seen before, private bits exposed. He looked down at his feet, and into the dust and brick. And he realized he was standing on his daughter's grave, and came off it, quick.

Johnnie shut the door on the bus, not believing what he'd just seen -- and in the same movement, he threw it open again and went back inside.

Bren looked at him as if he were no more than a curtain flapping in the breeze, or a fly come buzzing in. He ignored her, too, because he'd punch her in the face if he didn't. He went to Shirley, and he untied her.

'Let go that girl! Kath's been naughty to her mummy. Wait till her dad comes in!'

But it was all mouth. Johnnie was lifting the rope from round the girl's neck, and he was cuddling her, this little thing standing there like a stiff doll.

'Wet herself, didn't she?' Bren went on. '*And* never asked to go!' But Bren wasn't making any move towards them; either bored with being a mother or scared about what Johnnie might do. She picked up a cigarette stub and lit it, watching.

88

They'd found some little girl clothes from some-where, gypsy style. Shirley was out of her romper suit of the night before and was dressed in a short cardigan and a chequered skirt. She'd got some boots on. And she was wet through, at the back. Without thinking about it, Johnnie lifted her skirt and pulled down her soaking knickers, turned towards the door of the bus.

'Dry you out by the fire, eh?' he said.

All she did was stare at him, so he took her by the hand. He threw the wet knickers at Bren's head. 'You're loony, you are!' he shouted. 'You want locking up.' But he didn't wait to see what she did, was only sorry he'd missed her stupid face. He took Shirley and led her to the fire, where Biddy was giving a stir to a skillet of stew.

'Hello, sweetheart!' Biddy gave the kid a smile. 'Come to see me?' She made way for them. 'Careful, eh? Fire hot!' She kissed the girl on the head; Shirley only stood and stared. She was like something you moved about and could leave, a bendy doll. Smoke was going this way and coming that, but although a puff in the face made Shirley cough it didn't move her feet.

'She's got a wet bum, 'aven't you? Turn round, girl.' Johnnie turned Shirley, who went where she was twisted, for the back of her skirt to smoke itself out.

'You *are* a good girl!' Biddy put something into the stew from a screw of newspaper in her skirt, some herb, but not too much of it.

'Just do a lot of crying, don't you?' Johnnie, keeping

hold of her, patted her bottom to check on the drying, and found his mouth watering at what was coming off the pot. It had been a while since he'd had that boiled egg on the edge of the potato field.

'You eat here,' Biddy said. 'You've worked.'

Johnnie looked round at the bus.

'An' he's worked, the man, so her in there'll get a plate. But Granny Joyce says she ain't come out all day, so she'll have to wire in tomorrow, you tell her.'

Well, let stupid Bren blow, he'd be ready for a plate of whatever this pot was. Especially while over near the wagons some potatoes were being peeled, and onions and carrots being chopped. Whatever other way they lived, these gypsies had the right idea about first things first: good regular grub and somewhere soft to lay your head.

It wasn't dark yet, and not really cold if you were near this fire. There was a fluttering and twittering in the trees where the birds were saying good-night, fighting over the bed socks, as Johnnie's dad used to say. The little kids were still playing some game with a motor barrow up on a flat stretch of grass the other side of the road, and the older boys were stacking wood and slopping their heads in a bucket of clean water. And Johnnie was cuddling Shirley and drying out her skirt with a warm smell just this side of a singe. A bit peaceful.

And then came the knocking of a hard-worked engine, and the bark of running dogs, and Johnnie's peaceful moment turned to the twist of what was coming next. The *who* was Pricey and Christy and the men, coming back from the scrap; but it was the *what*, that was the pain. Pricey wanting a row with Bren? Or Christy wanting to prove who was cock of this heap?

Both, sure as eggs, the way life went.

Any road, the last thing Johnnie was going to do was move away from the fire, even if he could have said the words for Christy before they slopped out of his mouth.

'A load o' juvels! 'Lo, girls. Getting us supper?' He'd made sure Johnnie was in that bag, one of the girls: something to start a quarrel. Johnnie hugged Shirley again, turned her round to face Christy, like saying hello to uncle. 'See the big gypsy man?' he asked her. 'See that big mouth on it?'

Biddy stopped stirring, and Christy stopped breathing, ready for the kick-off. But Dukesey Joyce had come up behind and started ordering Christy to help off-load the scrap at the top end of the camp.

'I'll see you, mush!' Christy was all fist and teeth.

'Come on, warm those hands.' No doubt about it, Johnnie reckoned: he was his own worst enemy, always had been. Like his old dad, he didn't know when he was beaten. Always had to give as good as he got.

Biddy had gone now, over to the peeling. Johnnie picked up the little girl, and surprised himself how light she was. He carried her back to the bus, where he reckoned she'd be safer now that Pricey was about.

Bren was banging a saucepan around, scalding milk.

'She needs a dry pair of drawers,' Johnnie told her. 'You got any?'

'Dry drawers don't grow on trees. No more'n dry blankets do, and dry sheets.' Bren said it in a sing-song voice, with beats on *drawers* and *trees* and *blankets* and *sheets*, like a nursery rhyme she'd learned by hand over someone's knee.

'I'll ask that girl, Biddy.'

'I got some they give me.'

And now Johnnie looked, he could see the pile of children's clothes on the bed, crumpled where they'd come off bushes, but clean. He sorted out a pair of blue knickers, too big, but like a good 'un Shirley stepped into them and he tucked them over, round her waist.

'There. That better? Now, when you want to go, what do you say?' Johnnie turned the girl to face him. But she just stared back, as if no one was there.

'Pip, Squeak and Wilfred,' she said, in a voice from deep down in a dream.

'That's all she says.' Bren poured the browned milk into a jug. 'Stupid Pip, Squeak and What's-it!' She started breaking up hard pieces of that morning's bread, nearly spilt the lot as she took a hand away to tap her head, barmy. 'She ain't with us, that one!'

And Johnnie wished he wasn't as well. He left Shirley with a couple of pots and a cotton reel to play with and he pushed out of the bus. He took in a deep breath of smoky country air and he sighed it out big as he went to show himself – so as not to have Christy think he was yellow, or keeping out of the way. But he did wish himself a million miles off because what he knew was that come-uppances always did come up. What you were in for was what you always got.

He went to sort his bed. The bender tent smelt of the shed at the back of their house, where his dad had kept the tarpaulins that went over the loads and half-loads. Or, as he sniffed again, could be more a mix of the smell of their shed and of that barn at the farm, where the hay had come from. Whatever, Johnnie started to spread the stuff, and he laid one of the blankets on top, tried it for comfort and reckoned he could have lain cosy in here – if he hadn't got that fight to come; but he couldn't settle, couldn't sit still. He itched a finger down inside a sock, went at it vigorously, while his mind did its own scratching round.

Down his sock. That was a place, that was! Where the gold watch had been, where he could still feel it, like the ghost of the thing left behind. All these months later and he could still feel the lump of it. It was the gold watch that had done for him, had him being treated like some toerag little looter. And it didn't matter how much he'd gone on telling them it was all above board, him having the antique watch. It didn't matter how many times he'd said his dad could prove him right – that he'd paid cash for it, legitimate – for the simple reason, his dad wasn't *around* any more. He'd been marched off to some joining-up place two days before Johnnie had gone to school on evacuation day, him being looked after for a couple of nights at the woman's he had to call Auntie Pearl.

And what had she done to get him off the hook? Only looked down at her shoes as if the policeman might start staring into *her* cupboards if she opened her trap. His dad would have been very upset at her.

OK, the gold watch *had* been found down his sock at the evacuation parade, and it *had* been listed missing from the bombed-out tailor's shop in Fashion Street by the sister of the dead old cutter who'd lived there. But none of them accepted that the old man had sold it to his dad a week before, all above board; because there wasn't any ticket to show for it. The police were told to search through Johnnie's house for what he'd said to look for: one of his dad's blue books with the carbon paper. Because his dad never bought a thing without he got the seller to sign the book, and gave them the top copy. But the coppers weren't interested in that. They were looking for more stolen stuff, giving a dog a bad name.

A *tawdry little guttersnipe*, the woman magistrate had called him, *feeding off the victims of war*. He remembered those words, because they'd hurt. And then she'd told him how for the likes of him there couldn't be any normal evacuation, no billeting him with decent people. He'd have to go somewhere where real bad boys went. After all of which there was no one in the world who wanted to know when he told them that his dad just hadn't wanted the watch left in the house, to get stolen or bombed. He'd given it to Johnnie in case he never came marching home. The gold watch was what Johnnie had been left by his father. Like in a will.

It went without saying he'd written to his dad from approved school. *Private A. Stubbs*, care of Auntie Pearl — but who knew what she sent on?

He lay back on the straw and started to think how Christy might fight. Would he have any party tricks those *HMS Greengates* kids hadn't had? And the answer was, no doubt! Sure as eggs — remembering what Biddy had said about her father fighting to the death.

And he sat straight up as the girl herself put her head in his tent.

'They're going out after rabbits.'

He shrugged.

'He said, after they get back . . .'

'What?' But Johnnie knew all right. She didn't have to say.

'Over the road, on the flat. He'll fight you there.'

Well, he'd known that. Not the place, but he hadn't thought otherwise about the fight happening. He crawled towards the girl, went too far in the gloom and came close enough to feel the heat of the fire off Biddy's face.

'Has he got a caravan of his own?'

'No, he's not old enough for a wagon, that's for when you jump the broomstick. He's in the boys' tent.' Her eyes were asking *why?*

'You burn 'em in their wagons when they're dead, don't you? Gypsies? Would've been a waste of a good caravan.'

She sort of snorted, but it came out a very sweet sound. And it was funny how close her face always came; no one had ever had their mouth that close to Johnnie's. Now she looked as if she wasn't sure whether to back out or stay. 'You want me to tell him that?'

'Don' matter to me what you tell 'im.'

She made up her mind and came further in, and he had to give a little, while she balanced herself so she could stroke his face with her hand. 'You're too kushti to get busted up. What if I give him something? A make-peace, to give him best? Your belt, or a knife? It'd show, like a signal.'

'An' why would you do that?'

'I don't like people getting hurt. Especially . . .' She stopped. She was all breathing now, no words, didn't seem to want any.

He knew. She hadn't had to come to his tent, any of the kids could have told him about the fight. She liked him. She liked him a lot. And she was the sort to have anyone jumping the broomstick all right.

But now she was backing off, back to where she'd been before. She knew the answer to Johnnie giving anyone best.

'Well, you watch out, geyro. It ain't boxing, what our men do.'

And she went, and the tarpaulin flapped shut. And in spite of the smells coming off the cooking pot, Johnnie knew he wouldn't be eating more than just a spoonful tonight – to axle-grease his muscles, as his old dad used to say.

All the kids knew about the fight. The supper was all

eyes through the smoke and the two pairs meeting the most were Johnnie's and Christy's. Like prize fighters they did everything to show out as tough – tearing at a piece of bread, knocking back the tea so hot it fired the throat. And the kids stared from one to the other, with the food left on their plates. The thought of blood eats up the appetite.

Dukesey Joyce sat a bit apart on a stool he'd brought from his wagon; in his back pocket there was a catapult – big, polished, with a corded gripping shaft, red rubber dangling and a leather sling to it. 'There'll be a bit of moon. What ain't snared we'll stone.'

'You don't like rabbit stew?' the gran who'd led the potato picking asked Johnnie. 'It's rare good.' And she ate, but her eyes were on Christy, and on Johnnie again.

Pricey wasn't much part of the meal. He'd taken a couple of plates back to the bus, with a word from Dukesey which wasn't meant to be heard. Johnnie guessed what that was about. Bren was going to have to pull her weight tomorrow.

But that was tomorrow. Tonight there was going to be a fight.

At the finish – and no one left the fire without the word – it was a relief to stand to ease his legs stacking plates in the washing-up bucket. Biddy and the girls carried them off to the stream, while the boys played a half-hearted game and looked set to keep awake. While the men put their topcoats on and banged on the bus for Pricey; and with catapults, sticks, the dogs and a couple of shaded tin torches they went off the site on the uphill side – with Christy last, but not without that final word for Johnnie. 'Don't bother gettin' to sleep, geyro! I'll put your sparks out for you!' By which time the men were the shadows of trees, and Christy, showing a slice of strong teeth, ran to disappear with them.

Now Johnnie had to find that place behind the hedge, and quick! Where the nerves emptied him out like running water. Showing his backside to Russia, he washed himself, and when he'd notched his belt into a hole, he made his way whistling over to the fighting ground. Going to see what he could learn, but making sure he missed Biddy like the scarlet fever, in case she thought he was going off to hide.

Dukesey Joyce was right. A good moon was coming up, and by its spooky light Johnnie could see the lie of the fighting ground. It wasn't as flat as it looked from over the road. There were hummocks where rabbit holes had collapsed, and the grass was ringed by low gorse bushes, the sort that grew over Hackney Marshes. Which straight off had him wishing: of having the gypsy boy over in the prickles, face-down; then getting in on top and punching his head while he tried to get up. And pigs might fly.

He looked up at the face of the moon, clouds going across it like lacy bits on Auntie Pearl's line, giving a sort of slow wink down to earth. Like it knew things. Well, Johnnie knew things, too, and he wouldn't mind being all those thousands of miles away right now.

Which stopped him, had him turning to look as far

as he could across the fields. So why not run off again? Why hang about here to be beaten in for Christy to say he was cock of the heap? Why not just go, get off on his own? England was a blooming big place, and he wasn't born on a winkle barge, was he? If he was stopped, he could drag up some story about being bombed out, and losing his memory. He was good on making up stories, did it all the time round Aldgate. What was wrong with starting life up again over in Wales or Scotland till the war was over? When the war was over he could soon tail-lift it back to London for his dad coming home.

What did these people say? Kushti? Kushti and a half, mate!

He stood and stroked his face, the way Biddy had done. His hands were softer than hers, but your own didn't stroke so nice. A shiver took him over. If he didn't run, his old face was going to be in a right state by the time that moon went down.

He made out Biddy coming back from the stream, drying her hands on a big white rag, saw her look across, going boss-eyed to find him in the moonlight. He crouched down, didn't want to be seen; wanted to empty himself again. The rotten world was throbbing with the promise of a fight, and he was in it.

So why not go? Was he still crouching here only thinking about it on account of Biddy? What she'd reckon to him if he ran? What he'd miss, not seeing her again? He stroked his cheek again.

Which was when there was a thump on the side of the bus, and a scream, and Bren's voice suddenly shouting out of nowhere.

'You little tyke! You dirty little tyke!' And another scream, and another thump.

Johnnie was across that road in his boots as if they were White City sprinters – at the door of the bus and yanking it open before its springs had finished their rocking. Shirley, in her corner at the front, was standing, shaking, a scared little scrap. With a split lip where she'd been hit by something, and her chin and her cardigan were the yellow of milk and the red of blood. And Bren was coming down the bus, lifting the saucepan to her, so far out of her mind she seemed like something sent by Hitler.

'You drink! You don't spit! You dirty –' Her eyes were wild, her mouth was slobbering. And she was cracking down with that pot.

Johnnie grabbed at the quivering kid, dragged her out of that bus before the pot went crashing against the driver's window. And while the women and Biddy and some of the kids ran to the bus shouting, he took her up half under his arm like Pricey had and legged it for the trees.

7

THE BARN was right where he'd remembered it. Down the hill and up along a cart track on the way to Russia. Not that he could carry the kid all that way. After Biddy had stopped running after him and given over with her shouting, he'd put Shirley down and pulled her by the hand, trotting her with him, good as gold except for her screeching.

A dog barked in the farmyard, but the kid had stopped her noise as soon as she'd run out of breath, and Johnnie was in under the rut of the barn door well before the farmhouse could turn out. He stood leaning like a stick against the inside, hand over the girl's mouth, finger shushing at his lips while thick rubbery boots plodded outside. The barn door was rattled and a man's voice went on about 'ol' foxie', but he soon went back inside the house, still moaning.

Johnnie breathed again. He patted Shirley on the head for being a good girl, and he looked round to see what was what.

It seemed to breathe, the barn; it seemed to be alive. The hay piled high at one end gave off a sweet sort of heat and rustled like a great shaggy animal. A couple of harnesses hanging up seemed as if they still had the horses in them, creaking away. Old black cobwebs waved at every little puff of the air, and mice – or rats – ran about deep down somewhere, while an old roosting hen fluffed her feathers like Johnnie's dad sorting a bedspread.

The moon squeezed in through slats and made lines of white markers across to where Johnnie reckoned they'd sleep, on top of that indoor haystack. He'd never been a country kid; he played up and down cellar areas, not in and out of streams and on hayricks. But he saw how there were steps in the way the hay was piled, and putting up with a bit of scratching from the sharp ends he pulled and lifted the little girl up to a flat place out of sight of the floor, in against the back wall of the barn.

It would do him a treat. And the girl was what Biddy would have called real kushti. She didn't say a dicky bird, but it was like she knew he was helping her, that he'd pulled her out from being battered.

'You wanna do a wee or anything?' he asked her, before he tried to settle them both down for a sleep. 'Johnnie won't look.' But she just blinked at him.

'Well, I do, anyhow.' He went over to the far corner of the barn, and when he came back she was just as he'd left her, not a finger held different, still looking his way but as if she was seeing sweet nothing.

'Right, we're gonna get some kip, 'cos we're up and off 'fore they've got their socks on. OK?'

She stared at him, and he looked at her face in the scatters of moonlight. She was a pretty little thing, blue eyes and a nose no bigger than a dab of putty, and her hair could have been a treat if Auntie Pearl had got to it. Only the blood on her mouth took the edge off.

'Get yourself laid down, then, and I'll tuck you up under some of this.' He humped the hay into a sort of pillow as she lay, staring up at him while he scooped armfuls of loose ends across her. 'There y'are. Babes in the What's-it! Shut your mince pies – an' no calling out.' Johnnie leant over her, did a last bit of tucking in and, not able to stop himself, he bent lower and kissed her on the forehead. 'Night-night, God bless, cock,' he said. But she didn't reply; it was as if she was asleep already.

Getting himself settled wasn't so easy, though. It was a right restless business – but at last he was under his own thin layer of hay, settling for having a boot sticking out rather than rearrange himself all again. And he lay there and stared up at the rafters and the roof of the barn, listening to the creak of the night. But, sleep? He'd be lucky!

So what was he about? What was he going to do? He'd never get miles away to Scotland or Wales, not with this bundle. So what should he do with her? Because he had to get away. Leave her with the farmer while he got himself out of here, quick? It'd definitely set him free to do his own run, at his own top speed.

The little girl snorted in her sleep, but like with Biddy, it wasn't the ugly sort of sound old men did, it was more like a bit of a tune. He turned his head to look at her. No, mate, he couldn't leave her anywhere around here. Pricey and the gypsies would be claiming her back like one o'clock. They'd say she'd wandered off in the night, and she'd be back in with loony Bren by boiled-egg time.

So, *what*? Somewhere a way off he heard women laughing. It wasn't that late, could be land girls, wherever they kipped down, having a lark, still getting used to the country: come from all over – Aldgate, Plumstead, everywhere. No good leaving her with them. Land girls didn't have kids in their billets. They'd all be evacuated, or back where their mums came from.

So where the heck had Shirley come from? One minute Bren had been shouting for her rubber doll, then after the raid the kid had been tucked under her bedclothes. Which meant Bren must have stolen her from near Grandad Stubbs's yard: from Plumstead somewhere.

Which also meant – if he was going to do the kid any favours – he had to get her into a police station or some proper place where they'd send her back to her mum and dad. But, how – without getting nabbed himself? Little kids didn't always know their names and addresses. And into his head came evacuation day, all the Infants and the Junior boys and girls, all lined up ready to go with their little labels on. Yes! He could do it the way they had – easy – he could tie a message round her neck – 'Return to Plumstead'. Which seemed about the best idea. He definitely wasn't walking into any police station himself.

Right! Hunky-dory, so far. Then he could get himself off a tidy long way, hang out like a country kid till his dad came marching home.

He turned in the hay. Done it, hadn't he? He'd made his plan, and now he could get to sleep. If it went a treat, all right and good. If it didn't, well, he'd have done his best.

He rustled himself down, told himself those mice – or rats – were a long way off down below, they wouldn't come running up here. He could switch off for a bit. He knew he'd wake up early enough.

He closed his eyes on one long old day. He started to feel the pain of that potato picking warming out of his bones and down into the hay. And then for all that, Johnnie couldn't get off to sleep. He lay on his back, he lay on this side and he lay on that. He doubled his legs up and he stretched them out. But something was making sure he couldn't lose that bite of lemon in his gut. He could kid himself about making up his mind and switching off – but it didn't work. Something was still getting at him.

He watched the moon moving its markers slowly across the barn. The little girl, was that it? No, he'd sorted her out. He knew what he was doing there. Was it the whole thing of what he had to do tomorrow, get about, find food, dodge the law, get her into a nick? No again. He'd run before, and he was an Aldgate lad. He'd grown up doing those tricks.

So, what?

Well, he knew all right. He went through all the other stuff kidding himself, but he knew, sure as eggs. It was Christy. Johnnie Stubbs had run off from Christy. He'd grabbed the little girl and run quicker than you could blink your eye. He'd made running off with Shirley his excuse. Fair do's, he'd felt boiling mad about her; but what he'd done had been for him – and in his heart didn't he know it? From that moment of crouching on the fighting ground he'd taken the yellow belly short cut. He was getting out of the fight with Christy. And that was what was keeping him awake, because he wasn't proud of it – and someone else wouldn't have been proud of it, either.

The good thing is, you always go off to sleep in the end. Even down at *HMS Greengates*, at some stage in the night he'd stop worrying about tomorrow. And now it was the same in the barn. One second he had a real pain in his stomach, ashamed of how he looked to a girl like Biddy – and the next he was breathing deep with his mouth open, sound-o.

It was another bad night along the Thames. A 'bombers' moon' shone out unshaded, and the German air force navigators up in their Heinkels and Dorniers took the easy route to London, the crooked silver pointer of the river. And when these Luftwaffe got over their targets there was no need to drop flares to light up the oil storage tanks, the warehouses, the sugar refineries, the chemical works and the timber stacks. They were there as clear as day. The barrage balloons were up, but they could be seen miles off, and it was no hard job to keep higher so no wings were cut by their cables.

Reg and his watch had been called to the Woolwich Arsenal, where Britain's own shells and bombs were made, and it was taking one of its worst poundings of the war. As the incendiaries and oil bombs came down, the shrapnel flying around was more than German metal. It was twisted bits of the army's own stuff going up as well, and any second an unlucky hit on the 'Danger Building' – where the concentrated explosive was worked – could have half of Woolwich going to kingdom come.

Crews from five stations were in there, separated out and helped by the Arsenal buildings being a distance from each other. Miles and miles of hose ran and tangled in every direction. As one blaze was 'knocked down' by the firemen, the next scream of bombs started more, and strong jets of water turned to steam in a heat which grabbed into the men's mouths and scorched their breath out. White-hot cinders gusted in under the capes of their helmets, burnt into cheeks, lodged in eyes and ears, and the wet, slippery going turned knees and ankles as men battled to hold on. But in the furnace of it all, they were past worrying about themselves. Reg included. He might even have said yes to going up in this lot in one great bang. It would be the answer to everything, wouldn't it? With his Vera one of the living dead, and his little girl already blown to smithereens, wouldn't it get him back to both of them quicker than living through the rest of his miserable life?

'Got that in?'

Reg was connecting a line of hose to a taxi-drawn trailer pump. He'd been up at the nozzle for an hour, him and his mates, fighting to keep a steady jet on a blaze which had scorched his face London bus red. Now they'd been pulled back for a bit, to link hose along a line of trailer pumps to the river.

'In, and turned.' And the pump was run up into life, the hose filling like a long sausage, and the men crouching for a moment to draw breath, shrapnel pinging around like someone sniping.

Charlie Watson came over, bent double, pretended to give a hand. 'She'll pull out, your Vera,' he shouted, the next wave of bombers coming in up there and the anti-aircraft guns banging away. As a rule no one talked much about deaths and injuries, it was all 'get on with the job'. But Charlie had lost his mother not three days back, and he knew what was going on for Reg. 'You'll pull her round, talking to her, some favourite old song. Needs a tug, that's all.' There wasn't time to say more.

Reg crouched down on his haunches, pretended to look at a weeping hose connector. And in a sudden lull when the shouts up at the head could be heard above the explosions, he pulled out of his gaiters that scrap of paper he'd found from his bombed house. Something to read out loud to Vera . . .

And a sudden gust, it could have been the wind or the outside swirl of some distant blast, snatched the paper from his fingers and whipped it up into the air.

He jumped, he ran, he reached and he swore. But the paper was sucked into the upthrust of the fire they were fighting. He saw it curl and shake and burst into flames. If the heat hadn't already sucked every fluid from his face, he would have cried.

108

'Oi!' Charlie shouted. 'Come back here! Blow a ten-bob note, look to yourself!'

But Reg stood where he was and watched the glowing ember until it was sparked out, up in the cloud of black smoke. He came back to the trailer pump, his face a red mask, all eyes and blackened nostrils. 'It wasn't any ten-bob,' he said.

'Whatever it was . . .'

'A bit of a comic book.'

'Ah!' They turned to a shout from up the line, calling them to another pump.

'"Pip, Squeak and Wilfred",' he said to the din. And, under his breath, 'A bit of a favourite at home . . .'

Johnnie woke before the sun was up. He sorted himself out and climbed down the stack to look through the cracks in the barn. The moon had long gone, but there was a sort of country light coming in the sky, glowing over miles and miles of open fields. You didn't ever see it above the roofs of Brick Lane. In the flat pink of it he saw the farm and the kitchen, with a line of washing still left out, strung between the barn and the back door and blowing light against the dark of the farmhouse. The misery-guts air-raid wardens from Aldgate, like old Hewson, would have had them take that lot in. *You waving at Hitler, missus!*

He still felt mixed up inside. He was happy about what he'd do when he got on the road, but he was cut down over running from a fight. Which mightn't have got at him quite so much if he hadn't woken with

Biddy in his head; and it was her who had him feeling lumpy.

Some dream he'd had, and all! It had been him and her in those woods where they'd had their hard-boiled eggs, where she'd tried to back off from telling his fortune. Except they'd been on their own this time. And she'd kissed him: kissed him on the mouth. Kissing like that didn't come into Johnnie's life. Kids didn't kiss, that was for people on the films. In his dream he must have had his fight with Christy and won it, because Biddy was all lit up with him. He was sitting down and so was she, and she came leaning over him and pressed him on to the grass and gave him this kiss. Nothing got said, but she kept her eyes open and she wasn't heavy, and there was just this taste like golden syrup in his mouth. And he'd woken up dribbling, spitting chaff and feeling bad on account of it wasn't true.

A warm dream, turning cold. He looked at the frost all round the farmyard. He shivered and pulled his old jacket around him, wished it had all the buttons. Forget the dream, it was time he got away before the gypsies and Tommy Price came looking for him. He had to get a good few miles off before they started putting themselves about. And he was hungry, so he was going to have to do something about food pretty quick, for the both of them.

He went back to the stack and shook the little girl.

'Shirl! Shirl!' bending close to whisper it into the one little ear he could see. A chicken clucked at his voice, and something else did a scamper with a squeak

-- gave him a fright, coming a lot closer than he'd thought. 'Shirl, wake up, we're getting off.' He gave her another shake. 'Come on, we're off out of 'ere.'

She opened her eyes, looked straight at him. He was ready for anything: a screaming match, the waterworks. He was standing so he could grab her and run the way he had the night before, get away before the farmer came out. But her look was the same as if she was still asleep. She let him pull her up out of the hay and brush the stalks off her, and she took his hand to be helped down the stack like someone in a dream.

Well, he wasn't going to argue with that, it suited him, her behaving like a walking doll. 'Come on. We're gonna get off. I'll fetch us a bit o' breakfast. Then I'm gonna get you taken 'ome to your mum.' Did her hand shiver a bit in his? A scared lean back of her body? 'Your *real* mum, not loony Bren.'

And she looked his way, but through him. 'Pip, Squeak and Wilfred,' she said.

He got her to the ruts under the barn door, squeezed them both out under them, his legs ready to run when the dog barked. But it didn't. All he could hear was a bird giving off an alarm call. The dog must have been taken in. Johnnie had time to look round the farmyard to make up his mind which way to go. No decision to make. On his right, the washing line and the farmhouse. On his left, the gate and the road.

And Christy.

Christy standing like Hitler himself come for them, someone out of a nightmare in his long raggedy coat and his boots. High-voltage electricity shot through Johnnie, the biggest scare of his life; his body ready to fight or to run, but his buzzing brain standing him still, trying to sort the odds.

Christy standing still, too, but smiling, and Johnnie knew the gypsy could be over the gate and on them like lightning.

He shot a look at the farmhouse. What about a shout? Bring the farmer out? But whose side would he be on, with the gypsies working his fields? He'd be for one of them. And Christy still standing there, easing his bones ready for the fight.

Except, there was another picture in Johnnie's head. What he'd seen looking round. The farmhouse *and* something else. The clothesline: with a couple of farmers' shirts – and a woman's petticoats and knickers as well. And before Shirley could know what was happening, he pulled her back to run ducking under the clothesline – to the other side, a safe distance, where a gypsy boy wouldn't cross under women's clothes, not according to Biddy. And she'd been right. Christy was racing round the back of the barn to come at Johnnie from the other side.

Johnnie came fast back under to get on the safe side of the line again. He'd given himself some space, but this couldn't work for long. One shout and Christy could have the farmer out himself. Johnnie had no option but to run. He pulled Shirley with him, but he knew it was all no use. Christy running back round the barn again wasn't going to put a postage stamp between them in the finish.

He swore. But he went on running. He ran till his teeth juddered and his breath burned, half scooping the girl under his arm. But in less than half the first length of hedge, Christy was climbing the gate and coming on. Johnnie kept going, nothing else for it. He looked up and saw that the road running past the farm wasn't that far off any more, and he could hear a tractor. A bit of luck and he could just make it before Christy; and who knew what cart or farm worker or land girl might not be coming down there? Away from this farmhouse, he could always spin a yarn against a gypsy.

Which was when his right calf exploded in pain, dead-legged from behind. He went from run to hobble in half a second. He let go Shirley's hand and he twist-ed round to fight the kicker who was on him, some other gypsy who'd come out of the hedge? But all he saw was Christy back at the gate, his catapult up and aimed for the next shot. Johnnie had been stoned like some poached rabbit.

'Stop! You bide there!' The catapult was steady, and Christy was coming on towards Johnnie and the girl. 'You're comin' back wi' me.'

No fight, but surrender, hands up! Back to the site for Christy to get his pats on the back -- and the fight still to come, sure as eggs. The next slingshot was stretched at his head, a big black stone he could see from there. The first shot had nobbled him, but the next could kill him.

He could see Christy's teeth catching the light of the sun, a sneer turning Johnnie's stomach to hate

113

like milk goes to curdled bile. And Johnnie took himself by surprise, did something right off the wall. He let go Shirley's hand, stood up tall in the middle of the track and started flapping his arms, chicken style. He gave it the loudest, croakiest cockerel crow he could, along the lines he reckoned of Liney Silks.

Christy stopped.

'Come on! Chicken-licken! *I'm* cock of this heap!' He jumped to the side of the track, banked up by the hedge, then back to the middle. 'Chick-chick-chick-chick-chick! Can't fight without a catapult!'

At the thinnest edge it was a chance. Christy would either fight him for his cocky pride, or he'd keep his catapult aimed and march them back to the camp. Their eyes stayed fixed on each other down fifteen yards of dried mud. Somewhere the tractor throttled and birds were singing in the hedges; but nothing of all that was heard by Johnnie Stubbs. He'd slung a challenge on the frosty ground between them. Would it get picked up? Both of them were squinting. Both had their mouths shut tight. The only difference was Johnnie's hands held up like a boxer's and Christy's holding that catapult – with the rubber pulled as tight as it would go, the red of it stretched out to white.

When Christy suddenly threw the catapult down, stepped over it, and came walking on for Johnnie.

It was on. A street fight, without the kids in a ring and the shouting, but going to be a battle royal for all that. Johnnie had a hard little scar on his ear where he'd been bitten in this sort of roughhouse, and he would never stop catching it with a comb till the day he died – but he knew he'd come out of this with more. All the same, he squared up to Christy, who was walking in with his hands by his sides, going to do something sudden and hard. Johnnie's guard was the sort boxers took in fair fights. But they weren't stupid up Aldgate. Fights weren't only about boots and fists and teeth. They were as much about brains – so his boxing-by-the-rules stance was more to fool than fend anyone off. Johnnie was going to mix it like hell.

A boot came first, a sudden run at Johnnie and a flying kick at his groin, started in the air like a volley out of nowhere. But Johnnie had fooled him, by looking as if it was just his top half he was defending. He'd been ready to jump from the off, side or back, with his own boot up. Not quick enough for the kick to miss, but it didn't land with much force. It didn't hurt.

'Donkey!' Johnnie yelled. 'Chicky-chicky donkey!' He knew the value of working the other one up. Losing your rag got you careless. 'Chick-chick-chick-chick-chick!' He tried getting another flap and a crow in again, but Christy came like a shot-putter going across the circle, sideways on; and this kick did catch Johnnie off balance, and it did hurt him, up in his groin just left of the target, followed by the hardest punch to the side of his face Johnnie had ever taken in his life. Christy's fist was made of stone. It flashed lights in Johnnie's eyes and stopped him with his hands dropped. All he could do was shake his head, try to get back in focus before he took another one and went down for the kill. It kept him on his feet somehow, and through the bloody glint of his eye he saw the other fist coming in. The right, then the left, but the left one always a bit weaker. He ducked, made it slide off his cheek, and there was Christy's face, pulled forward on the ride of the punch and not checked by hitting solid.

Too close for Christy. Fried-egg eyes, open mouth, split-second frozen on their way to getting back out of it. Off balance enough for Johnnie to take his chance and bring up his good right knee, hard in the privates. Christy folded like a card table, couldn't find the breath for anything but a wild roar. He was as mad as a lion being red-hot-pokered. And he was on the further side of Johnnie now, nearer the road; and Johnnie had spotted what he'd thrown on the track in answer to the cockerel challenge. His catapult.

Johnnie grabbed it just as Christy saw the danger. He scrabbled for a flint, put it in the catapult and pulled it at Christy.

'Want it?' he shouted. He'd done it, was stretching the rubber fit to have Christy's head off.

Christy stopped, clutched at himself, sneering at what he thought of the rules being broken.

Johnnie told it to him, straight. 'All's fair, mate, where I come from. So get back home and put your nuts in a sling.'

For a flash of the eye it looked as if Christy might take a chance on Johnnie's aim, ready even to risk the flint in his face if it meant getting to Johnnie. But another pain grabbed him down below. He turned in

116

his double-over to look at Shirley, then he did what he was told and started hobbling up towards the road, like some old man. Just once he stopped and looked as if he might say something.

Johnnie followed the boy all the way to the road; and there he stopped. He called Shirley, who came, trotting, with those same wide eyes still seeming to see nothing. 'Come on,' he said loudly. 'You an' me's getting back to the farmer.'

Which he didn't mean, no way. That was to slow the gypsies when they came looking. He kept the catapult aimed at Christy's neck as the boy walked off up the road; and long before he turned round Johnnie was off in the other direction with Shirley – out of sight, running at a limp and rubbing his bad face, to find a village and unload her.

But he didn't hurt so much inside any more. He reckoned he'd sorted his yellow streak out; and now as he ran the taste in his mouth wasn't blood, but something more like golden syrup again.

8

JOHNNIE saw the next village when they came round
the bend in the road. The sun was higher now, glowing on a short street of houses below them on their
left. As they stopped and stood catching their breath,
they were about on a level with the chimneys, down
over the hedge and through the trees. They'd stopped
running a while back – Shirley's little legs had run
right out of steam – but he'd kept up a fast walk and
she was almost done in now. He took her over to the
side of the road where the frost had gone from the
verge, and he looked her up and down. She was a bit
of a sight after a night in the barn, a real little gypsy
in the old-fashioned skirt and cardigan, and they
might see some people soon.

So what did it matter what she looked like?
Whichever place down there was the village police
station, were they going to take more notice of a
bandbox walking in than a little scruff? If he couldn't
lay hands on a label or a piece of paper, so long as she
could say 'Plumstead', that's what counted.

'Here, you gonna say "Plumstead" for Johnnie?' he
asked her.

She looked at him.

'Eh? Say "Plumstead"?'

Still she looked at him, as if she'd been knocked

118

out in a fight and hadn't come right round yet.

'Eh? Shirl? Shirley? You say "Plumstead" for Johnnie?'

But all she did was turn, all of her own accord, and look on down the road like saying, *why aren't we getting on?*

'Johnnie take you to one of them 'ouses, and you say "Plumstead" to the man, an' 'e'll give you breakfast, an sweets . . .' But that didn't seem to mean much to her.

'"Plum-stead". "Plumstead",' he said, crouching down. 'Watch me mouth. "Plum-stead."'

And she did watch his mouth.

'Eh? "Plum-stead".' He could have won a speaking contest with it. And she was opening hers. He put on a face like someone getting a baby to say 'Dad'.

But, 'Pip, Squeak and Wilfred,' was what she said, in a voice like a speak-your-weight machine.

'Oh, you and that old stuff!' He walked on with her, her cold hand slipping in his. 'Lot of ol' nonsense, girl, i'n't it?' Then he'd just *have* to find a bit of paper and a pencil from somewhere and write his message; tuck it in her cardigan.'

Or, if he could find some old girl who wasn't up to chasing after him . . . He could give the kid over and *he* could tell her 'Plumstead'. Before he hopped it. Which wasn't a bad idea. He could get all ready to toe it, then tell the old girl, then go like the clappers down the street. *Good as done*, as his dad said. And as they got nearer to the village he could even see this old woman in his head: shawl, bent over, glasses, a

119

stick, and a hand on her bum as she hobbled along. And she'd definitely need to be different to the tough old birds they had on the gypsy site. Someone who wouldn't grab you, sure as eggs, with a grip on the wrist to strangulate the running of your blood.

And that being the top and bottom of it, they'd better clean themselves up, sort their faces and hands out. A sweet old girl would shoo them off double quick if she thought they were toerags. So Johnnie stopped, cocking his ear for something; and Shirley stopped, too, like a well-trained dog. He heard the throbbing of a tractor a few fields off, the stony clink of someone digging down in the village, and the chirping of the birds. But strain his ears till they hurt, he couldn't hear what he wanted – the sound of a stream.

'Come on, mate.' He slung the catapult away – didn't want to look like a poacher – and walked Shirley on. Then they'd have to see what they would see . . . And one moment it was a field, and the next they were down in the village street. No idea where. There weren't any signs up. Still, that didn't matter a lot to Johnnie. His geography wasn't up to much, anyhow. After a wash and getting shot of the girl all he wanted was a pointer to a big road going north.

The village looked like Dead Man's Gulch, no one about. And he couldn't hear the digging or the tractor the way he had before. Johnnie looked about him. Going by the light, it had to be about six or half past in the morning. You couldn't expect the place to be hopping yet awhile.

120

The church came first, all old stone, which could have been taken for a barn except for the spire. St Luke's, going by the noticeboard. Johnnie looked at it over its low stone wall. There were a good few graves around it for such a small village, old ones, big ones, and one with dead flowers still lying on it. But they didn't interest him; what did was something he'd spotted against the church wall. He took Shirley in through the gate, which squeaked out loud and had him hopping them in, quick.

'Come on, mate. They got a tap over there.'

There was a watering can and a tap, shown up from the road by the green slime down the wall. And, thank God, it worked! The water wasn't too keen to come gushing out. It dribbled down weakly and broke up into drops before it reached the ground, but at least there was something. Johnnie pulled a rag from his pocket, wet it and wiped over Shirley's face, gentle on the dried blood round her mouth.

'There y'are, little girl. Shine you up, eh? Could sell you off the front of the fruit stall!' He jollied her along, while he went to her hands and the grubby little knees which showed an inch between her skirt and her black socks. 'Cheers you up a treat. Don't know how you feel till you've had a sluice, do you?'

She didn't answer, took it, cold and all, without a murmur.

'Ain't got no towel. 'Ave to let God dry you. Shake yourself about a bit.' But she didn't. She stood and watched him while he did the same for himself, wringing out the rag as best he could and shoving it back in his pocket.

More for making sure than from any real hope, Johnnie went to the church porch and tried the door, a great black ring of a handle set in woodwork covered with metal studs. But it wasn't open. Not that he'd find anything to eat in there – and when had he last had his prayers answered? He led Shirley back through the churchyard and pushed an eye round the gatepost to look down the village street.

And what he saw coming took hold of his breath and set him in stone like one of those churchyard angels. A bloke in a leather flying jacket, and his first thought was *German!* Baled out after a dog fight, been walking the lanes in the night. But it wasn't. It was worse. As the sun caught him coming between two houses, Johnnie could see who it was, loping along like a wolf.

Pricey. Uncle Tommy Price!

Johnnie was back through that churchyard and dragging Shirley with him quicker than a rat on the run. He bent himself over and ran them for the porch; but at the last he thought better of that. If Pricey came into the churchyard they'd be well trapped in there. Instead he ran them round the side of the building and hugged them down tight behind the furthest wall.

And Shirley seemed to understand, as if she knew the rules of hide-and-seek. She hadn't seen who it was or she'd have screamed; but Johnnie's heart did enough of a dance for the two of them.

They were *all* out, then, the gypsies, not just Christy. They must have spent the night trying to find him and Shirley. Pricey was even taking a chance on being seen on his own by the Home Guard or the Military Police.

Johnnie could hear the footsteps now. Pricey's boots were those heavy army crushers, and the village street was a proper, hard road. And here they came, thud, thud, thud, thud. A bit of luck and they'd go on past and off up the hill where Johnnie had come from. But, no such! The loping suddenly turned to a scraping walk, and at about where Johnnie reckoned the gate was, they stopped – and the hinges did their squeak as the man came into the churchyard.

So had he seen them? Had they been too slow off the mark? If Johnnie had ever felt cold before, now he was huddled down like a little ice-man. He felt like something dug out from an Arctic cave, his cheeks and his mouth the most frozen of all, and he couldn't move a finger. And no sound from the boots any more, Pricey could be round the corner and on them any second.

Like now!

Or now!

Or now!

Johnnie wanted to shut his eyes on what was coming, but his frozen eyelids wouldn't let him. Down next to him, Shirley crouched silent and good – but she might as well have shouted or cried, because Johnnie knew this was the end of it.

But, twist, squeak, dribble and pat-pat-pat. And a

sucking off a hand, and a spit. Pricey was having a drink from the tap. He'd seen from the road what Johnnie had seen. That was all. But still Johnnie dared not move. Grass and nettles made noises when you kicked through them, and he wasn't risking that. The morning was as still and quiet as the dead-and-buried churchyard he was in, just a digging he could hear again. No point in trying to get further on round the church building. All he could do was hope.

After a God-awful silence, there was the rattling of that big ring in the church door, and a push. Johnnie could just see Pricey's shoulder going at it; and he hoped he hurt himself. More of a wait while life started to come back to Johnnie, feet upwards, paining him with pins and needles which he didn't dare stamp out. At the last, the blessing of that squeak of the gate again, like the hand of God on his head, and the boots on the road, going away.

Johnnie gave it a good count of fifty; then another thirty, because that was the easiest way to get caught, coming out too soon. And only then did he stand himself up and stretch against the rub of the church wall, crumbling bits off, and dare to put his head back round the corner. No Pricey – and no one else that he could see. All the same, they weren't going to come out that side, he reckoned, because if Pricey *did* do a turn-round, that was the side of the church to be seen from. He'd take Shirley on by the other side and get back to the village street over the wall; forget the gate. And then he could look out for his nice old country lady.

'Come on, mate, let's get you on your way . . .'

He took Shirley's hand again and found the least nettly way along the back wall of the church. It was all in shadow round there, damp up the walls and a smell like an Aldgate cellar; and there were graves to get round. No names that he could read, they were all in curly writing, and the stones were green and spotted with blobs of brown like camouflage. But he found a way over and through, lifting the girl when he had to, and giving her little jumps.

At the far end of the churchyard there was a hedge, and another small gate, leading to a field. Johnnie couldn't see over, but when he got them to the gate – a tricky little go-in-and-go-out affair to fool the cows – he could see how the field ran down behind the houses; with old sheds at the back roofed in curly red tiles, a whole line of them.

Which meant that with a bit of luck he could find his dear old lady in her own back garden and not have to show himself in a shop or knock at a front door . . .

He pushed the gate and squeezed Shirley in the gap with him. He closed it behind and went on into the field. So, they'd aim for that line of sheds and see if they could get to a back door for knocking on.

'You can halt right there! I've been watching you, boy!'

Stone the crows! Who needed Hitler to give you frights? At the back of the hedge was this woman holding a garden fork at him, a tall party in long horse-riding boots and slacks tucked in, with a big jumper like a roll-top desk. She had a load of hair piled up under a hair net so thick you could go shrimping with it, and she was all face-powdered, with a slash of red lipstick on, even this early in the morning.

'Who goes here – eh?' Johnnie stood still, holding Shirley's hand and trying to crack a smile on to his face. No chance.

'Who are you, skulking round the churchyard? Have you got identity cards?' She was a lot older than Auntie Pearl, and her voice was posh, as if the king and queen went regular to tea. 'Papers? What proof are you carrying – and where are your gas masks?'

'Only having a look about,' Johnnie said. A cat could look at the blessed king.

'To what end?'

'Eh?' Keep her gabbing, and think about which way to run. She couldn't grab them from where she was, not without treading over where she was digging. And she might get the kid but she wouldn't get him.

'You're not from Little Farrow?'

'No, miss.'

'So . . .?' The woman had been at a row of greens, a titchy allotment down the side of the hedge, and her own gas-mask box was hanging on a spade down at the other end. 'Your sister?' Her eyes were beading into him, then into Shirley.

Johnnie nodded.

'Well, there are no flowers here for hawking round the county.' Her nose was dribbling, but she was the sort who took no notice of an item like that. 'And you can tell your people what I said.'

'Who?'

'Your Romany lot. You can all keep your gypsy hands off other people's property, understand? We don't want your sort round here!'

Johnnie stoppered his lips up tight. *Nothing useful to pour, keep the top in the bottle*, was what his dad always said.

'Now, get off out of the village. And if I see you back here I'll report you for unlawful ingress.'

She had to be a teacher or a judge when she wasn't digging for victory. 'Come on,' Johnnie told Shirley. He could have said more, but right now he wanted her to go on thinking he was a gypsy.

He took Shirley back through the gate into the churchyard and came to the start of the village street, the woman watching them all the while. He went left, to go down past the row of village houses. He definitely wasn't backtracking up the hill the way Pricey had gone; so they'd go on down the street and out the other end.

And he'd have to forget his dear old lady for a bit.

He led Shirley on the sunny side, kept his free hand stuck as cocky as he could in his pocket and put a bit of a gypsy swagger into his walk. He took a leaf out of Dukesey's book – how he led his horse. Head up, he walked Shirley past the row of houses, past the country bus stop and the letter box in a wall, past the village shop, and he went on walking to where the fields started up again, with hedges both sides of the road. He wasn't going to stop till they came to the next place the bus went. And as he walked and Shirley trotted, he thought about how the woman had taken them for gypsies. And it came into his head that it might be favourite not to drop Shirley off too quick. As a boy on his own, he was a boy on his own, wasn't he, no identity card, no gas mask – could easily be someone on the run? But with the girl alongside, looking like a little Biddy, they could be brother and sister totting for scrap. Which might get them a toe-ing as gypsies, but no one was going to think, *HMS Greengates* and phone the School Board. And the more he thought about it the more common sense it seemed. He could get them a bit nearer to the road to Wales or Scotland before he left Shirley with a ticket to Plumstead.

He looked down at himself. Old jacket, scruffy trousers, hard boots, the outside getting on to his face thanks to that bruise; he was getting on for being a dead ringer of Christy. He put his hand to his throat. Just the one extra thing . . . He tugged the damp rag out of his pocket and tied it round his neck the way the gypsy men wore theirs. What was it, his diklo? Well, it suited him, he reckoned. He felt the real Dukesey Joyce. And wouldn't he have liked Biddy to see him!

'Come on,' he said. 'You 'ungry?'

Shirley looked at him, didn't answer, but she had to be. Plus there was this great hole in his own belly. So it was breakfast for two. He looked along the empty road and over the hedges, fields going up to a wood on one side, and country all the way to Russia on the other. Now, then – where was he going to find some grub?

Vera Lewis was taking liquids by mouth, but that was all that was going in. However close Reg leant and whispered, however hard he squeezed her hand, there didn't seem to be a thing she was understanding. Helping out the nurses by giving her broth from a cup, Reg slid shallow spoonfuls in and lifted her chin after each one to close her mouth. Then Vera would swallow, and he'd gentle her mouth open again. Well, at least this was an improvement to feeding on the drip.

They were down in the basement now. St Nick's Hospital was no more than three-quarters of a mile away from the Woolwich Arsenal. For the last couple of nights bomb blast had shaken the place like a tenement in an earthquake, with the bedridden down in the basement now, joined by the walking wounded when the siren went. And Vera was the most bedridden of those still alive.

The basement was dark and crowded, damp and disorganized. The internal doors were sandbagged against blast, and the bags gave off their own sour smell. But it was safer than the storeys above.

'Come on, Vib, one more mouthful.' It was like coaxing a last spoon into sleepy Shirley, and Reg's eyes welled up at the thought; his chest shook, and the spoon dribbled the broth down Vera's chin and neck. 'Sorry, love,' he said, and he got hold of himself, the way firemen had to.

Sister came past, the big one who seemed to have a

bit of time for him. She went past the foot of the bed, then turned back, all in one movement.

'Keep it steady, Fireman!'

Reg gave her a pale grin.

'She's just about holding on,' she said, 'thanks to Our Lady.'

Reg rested the spoon back in the cup. 'Every day's one more.' A fire-smoked croak.

'It is. But now we're looking for that next step, aren't we? The body is still working, but now we want the brain.'

Reg looked at Vera, who seemed so peaceful. As he'd done for twenty-four hours, he thought of the tragedy of her dying, and the tragedy of her staying alive.

'The boys on the watch reckon she needs a prod,' he said. 'Some song, or words she'll remember under all that sleep . . .'

'And I've known it work.' Sister straightened the blanket.

'Only wish I could see in her head.'

She nodded. 'A bigger mystery than the pyramids. She could be hearing every word we say, and taking everything in; and still she won't be letting herself come out.'

'Won't?'

'Because we're not telling her what she wants to know.' She bent lower to Reg so she didn't have to shout. 'Because her poor brain's in there telling her she'd rather carry herself off than wake up without her child . . .'

130

Reg put down the cup without looking.

'I've seen it with conscious people, too. In the last lot. Shell-shock – hundreds clammed up altogether and others starting up talking gibberish. Bless us, it's the brain's way of not letting the body take any more hurt.' She looked round. 'Now don't you sing that to Doctor. I can talk straight to you . . .' She went, stepped over a fire bucket and round a locker.

Reg looked after her, then he came back to Vera; checked round the basement himself because this was going to be private. He leant forward; checked again.

'If you can hear me,' he told her, down in his throat, hardly any breath to carry it on, 'I don't half love you, Vib.' He squeezed her hand, and kissed her cheek – and felt very bad because even as he was saying it, his head was really filled with a picture of Shirley. Not just for him, of course, it was for Vera, too; thinking how her brain might give the all-clear and her eyes light up if their little girl were still alive to be held over the bed for a kiss.

But that was a pointless thought; and he sat back, and stared at the past in Vera's face.

9

FOOD. They'd faint without food. They'd drop down weak and feeble in a ditch and get caught, not having the fuel to fight or to run. But as they'd gone out of the village and turned on to something a bit wider it struck Johnnie how being hungry was making him lose his edge. First off, he'd been all eyes for the road and all ears for the sound of the scrap lorry or the clopping of a bareback horse. Now all he was skinning his eyes for were berries in the hedge or an apple left on a tree. He was getting pulled off his main business. *Keep your mind on your job*, his dad always told him, if he started mooning when he should have been mending. *That's how you end up with a thumb and three fingers*. So he had to get on, all eyes and ears again, and blow his empty belly. Food there was, in *HMS Greengates*.

But in the end Shirley put the brakes on. In the middle of a bend she just stopped, and sat down. Right there. Like a heap of old clothes dropped off a tailboard.

'Come on, mate, not much further.' He took her hand to pull her up. But he'd been saying 'Not much further' all the time; why should she believe him now? She sat there, and she stared ahead.

'*Shirley!* Car might come.' No movement, no

coming with his pull. 'A lorry.' Or going with his
push. 'Ten tanks and the Flying Scotsman.' But she
wasn't budging, not short of being lifted, and Johnnie
wasn't up to that, nor a screaming set-out. Already he
was changing his mind, ready to get shot of her,
quick.

'Right. See that house? I'm gonna knock there and
get us some breakfast. Something to eat.' He mimed
it, shovelled forkfuls into his mouth and rubbed his
belly. 'Lovely grub. Eh?'

She still wasn't moving. He looked up at the sky. It
had to be time for country people to be up.

He left her where she was, sitting in the middle of
the road. The house wasn't far and he reckoned he
could chance it.

It seemed funny, the house, out there on its own. It
was thin, like being built for squeezing into the
streets of London, not for out in the country.

A last look back at Shirley, sitting in the road like
an Infant in school prayers, and he opened the stiff
gate. As he walked up the path he saw that the front
garden was all vegetables, another one digging for victory, like the government said to do. Ahead of him,
the windows were so dark the curtains could have
been open or closed – and the front door looked as if
it wasn't just closed but painted shut, dust all down
the crack. He reached up and lifted the heavy door
knocker, let it fall with a thud that had him half-way
back down the path. He looked round. Shirley had
come to the front gate, was standing there sucking
her thumb.

And someone was coming down the passage from the back of the house; nothing Johnnie could hear, but a sense, a slight change in the feel of the place. And as he stood facing it, the door opened.

The man looked more scared than he was. His eyes went out over Johnnie's head as if he'd been knocked-down-ginger by German paratroops.

'Uh?' The man saw Shirley at the gate, and Johnnie now. It was hard to tell how old he was, his hair could have been fair or it could have been grey, he didn't have a whisker on his face – hardly even an eyebrow.

'Dukesey Joyce the gypsy. My dad. 'E's coming round behind,' Johnnie told him, out of nowhere. At which the man's mouth dropped open and he stared out again, more frightened of a gypsy up his garden path than a German. Johnnie played on it. 'Won' be long. You want any sharpening done? Knives, scissors, nail files . . .?'

The bloke looked as blank as the wash-house wall: his face, and the rest of him, too. So wishy-washy to Johnnie, he put him in mind of a picture in a colouring book before you'd got your crayons to it. Now he was shaking his head, trying to shut the door.

''E'll give you a knock, Dukesey.' Johnnie's boot was on the threshold.

Another shake.

'He will – if you like. 'E's coming right past 'ere in a bit.'

A drop of panic went into the closing of the door.

'Fair enough, then. I'll tell 'im.' Johnnie had heard

of a gypsy's curse; he should have asked Biddy how you gave it. The man gave a little sigh, like being let off. But Johnnie had only just started his fast shuffle.

'Oh, 'fore you go – you couldn't spare us a crust an' a drop of cow juice, could you? Only, we got no food, an' Dukesey 'ad to give us his boot instead of breakfast. He'd think that real kushti.' He wanted his gypsy dad sounding a real rough who might just be smoothed down by someone being kind to his kids.

The wishy-washy man didn't like this one bit. His mouth puffed in and out like a dying goldfish. 'Bide there. Don't you come in,' he said, which even in all the quiet Johnnie had to stretch to hear. He went down the passage and into a room at the end, closing that door on himself. Johnnie did a thumbs-up for Shirley.

'Told you – breakfast,' he said, and she came up the path and into the porch like a puppy called to the bowl.

The man came back, quickly now, to have them go. He carried a large enamel mug, a loaf and a bread knife. And without a word, and still with his eyes outside for the dreaded Dukesey Joyce, he gave the mug to Johnnie. It was well filled with thick country milk. Johnnie had first sip in case the girl spilt it, then he held it for Shirley. She put her lips to it and drank, while he tipped it. And Gordon Bennett, was she thirsty! ''Ere, 'alf-time!' He had some more himself, while the man started cutting a couple of slices of crusty bread, holding the loaf to his chest and sawing inwards.

135

They both ate the bread standing there. Not fresh, Johnnie's top slice had a real hard edge to it. But it was food, it went down well; and with it came a pain in Johnnie's bowels.

It was the sort of spasm that kept you rooted while you rode it out. 'You wanna go to the dubs? The lav?' he asked Shirley. And she nodded. 'She wants to go to the lav,' he told the man, looking round at the road to give the lie that Dukesey Joyce would be there any second. 'Go 'ere, can't she?' And back to Shirley. 'Won' take long.'

The man was not at all happy about this. He looked like one of those customers Johnnie's dad used to string along, when he added little items to the bill for this and that.

'You better be nimble, then.' A quick look out and the man brought them into the house and shut the front door. He shuffled them down the passage, through a back parlour stuffed with armchairs Johnnie's dad would have dribbled at, and out into the scullery. He shooshed them through to the back yard and round to the privy, which leant against the wall of the house the way Johnnie's did back in Woodseer Street.

Johnnie helped Shirley in – to a low wooden shelf the whole width of the privy, with a big hole in the middle.

'You be all right?' he asked. 'Don' fall down to Australia!'

Shirley said nothing, but shut the door on Johnnie, who stood and waited.

'You sure there ain't nothing you want sharpened?' he asked. 'Kitchen knives?' He knew knives were about. He'd nearly hoiked one up his sleeve coming through the scullery, a handy-looking job on the draining board, except the gold-watch business had taught him a painful lesson.

The man looked at Johnnie, or all round him, you couldn't be sure. He shook his head.

''E's a right big bloke, Dukesey Joyce. Could sharpen a plough, if you want.'

Another nervous shake of the body, which rattled the man's eyeballs. And Johnnie felt pleased. This was working a treat, being a gypsy boy.

Shirley couldn't pull the chain. She couldn't reach. She came trotting out, putting her skirt straight.

''Ang on,' Johnnie said, and went inside himself before the man could stop him, latched the catch over and sat down himself. He wasn't long. He'd got used to not dwelling since *HMS Greengates*. Just time for a look at the wall, where a 'Spot them in the Air!' poster was stuck on the plaster, showing silhouettes of German planes. So the bloke sat here scaring himself to death! Crapping himself! And Johnnie grinned at his own joke. But no messing about, people being scared – you could play on that a treat.

So he kept it up for the wishy-washy man, right to the last knocking. ''E won' be more'n a couple of mo's,' he told him as he took Shirley down the path. 'Listen out for 'is motor.' But the door was shut and a bolt was slid before they'd taken two steps.

'Come on, mate,' Johnnie told the girl. 'Best foot

forward. Then swing the other one. You're getting back to your real mum and dad.'

And she toddled with him, dead slow but good as gold. While the fields came to life with tractors and ploughs; and bikes and a post van passed on the road; and someone walking the other way crossed over, out of their gypsy path. They hid in a ditch when a horse and cart came their way, and a salvage lorry had them down behind a hedge. They stood to attention and Johnnie touched his collar when a khaki Red Cross ambulance passed them in the lane, driven by a woman soldier. But they got on while the sun came up in the sky; and please God in the right direction. There wasn't a step, though, when he wasn't on the look-out for a good place to drop her. She took three or four little steps to every one of his, and she wouldn't last the pace for long. And she wasn't much company, either. She kept her pretty little face pointing the way they were going, with her eyes open and her mouth shut. When there was a scare and he pulled her, she went quick enough, seemed to know he was all on her side. But that was about his lot: everything else was all shut out. Who knew what was going on in her brainbox?

He walked her on. Fair enough – he had enough going on in his own brainbox without getting the jitters over her. Sad things like hearing his dad's voice in his head, coming out with all his old sayings. And the thought that hit him like high explosive, seeing that Red Cross ambulance for wounded soldiers – what if his dad had got killed? He was a soldier

138

somewhere, wasn't he? Could be fighting the Germans right this minute. And soldiers did get killed. What'd be the use, then, going up north or over to Wales, and coming back when the war was done if his dad never came marching home? A thought which Johnnie shut his eyes at and nearly had Shirley into a hedge. But it had to be faced out. He could have seen the last of his dad. In which case, he'd have to stay away from London for ever, because there'd be no one in the world to clear him of the gold-watch business.

Miles away in thoughts like that, he walked the girl on, wandered all over the shop, as his dad would say. Till he suddenly stopped in the middle of the road – and Shirley with him, like a good little dog.

Why go up north at all, then? Or over Wales? Why not get shot of the girl and *sort out the watch business himself*? Like he'd been going to do first off? Why hang on for the end of the war?

He walked them on again, quicker, made the girl trot. Get back home to Woodseer Street, that was favourite again – and find what he knew was in the front room in his dad's little cupboard. The duplicate books, the one with the page the rotten police couldn't be bothered to find. Sort out the dead tailor's name where he'd signed for selling the gold watch, and march it down the town hall. Clear his name.

He picked up a stick and threw it over a hedge. Yeah! He knew how to get into the house, no problem over that. He knew the weak window catch like an old mate. He could blitz his own place, easy. So all he needed now was a nice kind face for handing over

Shirley, and a good pointer to the right road for London.

'Tell you what we're gonna do . . .' He told the plan to Shirley, made it sound like some adventure story. But if she was old enough to understand, she didn't show it on her face. She looked at him and blinked. And didn't say a dicky bird.

All he needed was a shop or a lady in a garden where he could hand her over, say 'Plumstead' and run. But nothing ever seemed to come round the next corner – except the next corner after that. Nothing like a village or a little run of houses. Just farmers' gates leading to yards and barns, and a pub with No Gipsies written on the door. He kept on past all these places, holding Shirley's hand till it got hot, then swapping to the other one.

'So who's this ol' Pip, Squeak an' Wilfred?' he asked her, thinking she might come round to talking sense again; but she just said the names in a sing-song voice, and kept trotting on. At least she wasn't pulling against him, he told himself, or running off, or going on with a load of whiny questions. That was something, till the parting of the ways.

By now the sun was getting up quite high. For an October day it was warm, and Johnnie's limbs felt free and oiled. On one stretch of straight road he suddenly did a little tap step on his metal blakeys and started up with a song.

'You are my sunshine, my only sunshine,
You make me happy when skies are grey,

140

You'll never know, dear, how much I love you,
Please don't take my sunshine away.'

And it was sung to Shirley, with a little dance around her; and she gave him the start of a smile, just the start. And when he took her hand again to get on up the road it was a tighter little hold, could almost have been a squeeze.

''Ere we go, girl!' he told her, the skip still in his step. 'You for a nice lady an' Plumstead. An' me for Woodseer Street!'

'He ain't gone far, because he ain't magic. Vanishing off the face of the earth's a mulo trick, not human.'

The scrap lorry was blowing out more black smoke than the burn off an oil bomb. It whined up the hill, threatening with every turn of the wheels not to make it, but Dukesey Joyce sat in the cab with the look on his face that said the lorry was the least of his worries. He had Tommy Price next to him, and it was the soldier who was getting his scowl. 'The boy's *got* to be hiding up local.'

'I looked all night. Ain't 'ad a drop of sleep for looking.' Tommy Price stared out through the windscreen. 'Just never searched no barns to get blown off the end of a double-barrel!'

'Well, that's where he was, 'fore he korred Christy for breakfast.'

'Little basket!'

'Any road, it's not just the boy – it's the both of them.'

'Where *he* is, *she* is.'

'Right. An' you'd better find 'em or we'll all finish up in prison.'

Tommy Price lit a cigarette, offered one, to have it waved away. 'Don't see it, do you, you ordinary people? How's it go?

> 'My mother said, I never should
> Play with the gypsies in the wood . . .

'What they sing to their children, wi' the idea we run off with their babies and sell 'em.' Dukesey Joyce topped the hill with the old lorry and pushed it into another gear, gripping the steering wheel tight. 'You've been round the cooking pot. You ever seen kids better loved?'

Tommy Price flicked ash on the floor of the cab, looked deadpan at the road ahead. Love never much came into his scheme of things.

'Lives for his kids, the gypsy does, worships 'em, sets 'em a sight higher up the hill than you set your'n.' He took a bend too fast, slid himself into Tommy Price along the bench seat, swore. He put the lorry right. 'Now you get this, 'fore that boy blabs his mouth on our Brenda Lee –' he found a straight enough road to poke Price's forehead with a finger – 'I want that baby found. *Where'd* she come from?'

Tommy Price rubbed off the poke. 'Blown in by a bomb, 's what Bren says.'

'Orphan, then?'

'Suthin' like that.' Tommy Price snuffed his smoke and saved it.

142

'Well, I tell you what I want. I want her back up the road in my wagon 'fore that boy gets her to someone who'll fault us out an' move us off our site. I want her treated right and *known* to be treated right. I want her loved proper, and never knocked around the place again. I want her growing up *wanting* to be a Joyce kid, an' I want that boy knowing it.'

Tommy Price shrugged.

The lorry stopped so suddenly Tommy Price hit the wind-screen with his head. When he turned to swear, Dukesey Joyce's face was an inch away. 'So we find em, soldier boy, or you'll be back in the army Guard Room 'fore your spit dries on the road.'

Tommy Price looked out past where his head had hit. They had come to the dividing of the roads just outside the village where the church was. Dukesey Joyce racked up the handbrake like tightening a noose on a rabbit. The lorry started throbbing, made Price's cheeks go with it.

'Where they off to, then? Heading back to London?'

Tommy Price nodded. 'Got to be favourite.'

The gypsy's speech had never been so slow. 'Right you are, then. We just get our horses after 'em.' He meant the lorry, and revved the juice while he found a forward gear. 'An' we ain't goin' back on our own.'

Tommy Price looked to the road on his right, and to his left. 'Which way you goin', then?'

'Every way till we find 'em, or I'll turn you in myself 'fore I take the blame. The military finding you won't be too hard a job.'

Tommy Price spat out on the road and looked up at

a signpost with missing arms. 'Which way's for London?'

'This time o' day, keep the sun on our right.' The gypsy let his boot off the clutch to take the lorry down the right fork. 'But we'll cover every inch of the county if need be.' He took the first downhill bend at a rare pace. 'We'll go all round the moon and stars, but we got to be quicker than a kid wi' a toddler along.'

10

SHIRLEY was toddling so slow Johnnie would have to be rid of her before he grew any whiskers. Especially with the real chance that Dukesey Joyce could be along any minute – him or Pricey, on the chase. At one farmer's gateway, standing back for a tractor to come out, he put Shirley on his back to make up a bit of time. But she seemed heavier now, and she didn't have the knack of hanging on tight. His eyes were skinned for the sensible lady he could say 'Plumstead' to, and hand her over.

He passed a cottage and half decided to knock and off-load her there; but he didn't have a good enough feel about it. *Beware of the Dog.* There was always the chance there'd be something better round the next bend. And if not the next, then the one after that. One lane led to another, and into a wider road at another unmarked crossroads. Here the trees were painted white to the height of his head, for cars to see the edge in the dark; which said this could be a main road to somewhere.

He followed the trees, looked down at Shirley. She was starting to drag her feet, tired and hungry again.

'Not far. We'll have a rest. Find some grub.' *And* a nice old lady, he thought – if Anyone Up There's listening!

Which was when they passed the school.

Not that it looked like a proper school at all. To Johnnie schools were as big as castles, all turrets and high railings and shouts and whistles. This one was small, more like a little church with its holy-shaped windows, but a school it definitely was, because there was a small yard of children come out to play, the other side of a low wall.

He held Shirley back a bit, behind him, didn't want anyone seeing them and shouting 'Gypsy!' Not if it wasn't going to pay off. He crouched with her till he was sure no one was staring, then he crawled forward and looked again. Behind the kids coming out he could see a full milk crate in the porch, with some sort of a kitchen tin laid by it. Powdered egg or potato, needing boiling water? Well, that wouldn't be a load of use to him – but balanced on top of it were four shiny round tins about twice the size of a big pot of jam; no labels on, but stamped with blue numbers. And he knew what they were all right. Tins of malt, the stuff they dolloped out in spoonfuls: tasty, and good for you. One of those would last him a couple of days when he'd got shot of Shirley, iron rations. If it wasn't too much grief to carry.

Still keeping Shirley behind him, he looked harder at the children between him and the tins. One or two were his sort of age and the rest were younger, with a few real babies. But they were not the same as the kids from his own Wicks Street School, these with their navy-blue raincoats on, and their school caps, and scarves criss-crossed and wrapped around, playing gallopy-gallopy games. He kept low behind the wall and looked for the teacher, but there wasn't any sign. Having a cup of tea inside, no doubt. And that was different, too. They had them out like guard duty at Wicks Street.

'Shirley, wait here!' he told the girl; and again he wasn't too happy about the gypsy look. He wasn't going to merge in too well with this raincoat lot, looking like a totter. Although, when he screwed out all the corners, he did spot one or two scruffs among the country kids.

Anyway – he was going for it. He did a little run back along the wall to where there was a gate at the side; and with a last look down the road for danger, he slipped himself into the yard. Joined in, straight off – started galloping like the worst of them, smacking his own bum and holding a rein like Roy Rogers the film cowboy, going round in circles and clopping his mouth for horses' hoofs. And two or three dodges and the odd funny look; and there he was at the crate in the porch. The door into the school was open a crack – no one inside looking out – so one quick lift and he had a malt tin off the crate and was galloping back for the gate.

To be choked by a tug at the back of the scarf, sudden and fierce – hoiking him off his feet and down on the ground, all in one swing.

'What you up to, gippo?'

It was one of the bigger boys, blue mac and school cap – and definitely not the softie. The cap was twisted like a Spitalfields porter's and the face was about as sweet.

'Get off!' Johnnie tried to get up, but another kid was already on him – and a hard-looking girl had the tin from his hand. Both London tough.

Johnnie humped and twisted, kicked and squirmed like any East End boy. And he fought himself to his feet. But just when he was going to run for it a big old man in a waistcoat gripped him hard by the muscle, something worse than Old Nell.

'Tyke!' he was shouting, farmer-faced, as if Johnnie were a snorting bull. 'Thieving tyke!' And he smacked him round the face and sent him across the yard like the wrong end of a knock-out. 'You tell your thieving people I've got my evacuees to feed here. London kids. Proper cases! You tell 'em that . . .' And he was coming to give him another one. Except that Johnnie was back through that yard and over the wall, a couple of Infants bowled over and crying in the escape. No time for collecting Shirley but across the road and over a gate into a field, and off along the line of the hedge like an Olympic runner. Till the shouting started to fade, and a whistle blew for the end of playtime.

Pulling breaths of fire down into his lungs, Johnnie hunched himself under the prickles. His eyes were watered out dry, his nose poured into his mouth, and he coughed up his life. His heart gave his jacket a push from inside, till he could slowly stand up and start feeling his teeth to see if he still had a full set. And when he knew that he had, he bent forward to a stretch where he could look over, and back up the road. All at once it wasn't Johnnie Stubbs he was worried about.

It was Shirley.

Where the hell was she?

She hadn't followed, and she wasn't where he'd left her. The school was a good few barge-poles away, but he could see its low wall, and Shirley wasn't there where she'd been left.

He spat the blood taste on to the ground – except it wasn't red, only boiling spit – and he bent over, finished, and he swore. He'd lost her, then, going for the malt. Lost her into the school. Barney Bull had chased after him and seen her down by the wall. And he'd have had her, as sure as eggs; with no one to say 'Plumstead' to him. And if the best she was saying was 'Pip, Squeak and Wilfred', she'd never get home, not in a million years. Someone had to do her talking for her.

He crouched behind the hedge; stood up again and looked once more, hoping wildly that she'd be there this time. Her little dimply legs showing between the skirt and the socks, her pretty little face looking at him, wanting him to go and get her. But there wasn't a sign; and he sank back and rubbed the pain in his belly. Which wasn't hunger this time, but the rotten feeling of losing.

Back in London it was a fact of life that certain sorts of people did certain sorts of jobs. According to Reg, landlords in pubs always made you feel that a Lonsdale Belt for winning at boxing was hanging up just the other side of the cellar door. Then there were bus conductors, the comedians who hadn't made it

149

onto the stage. And there were the people who did the thick-skinned sorts of jobs – like the slaughter-house men, and this man here in charge of the wartime mortuary.

Reg was at the public baths, closed for swimming due to the need for somewhere to store so many bodies while they made up the daily Civil Casualties list. And this morning a quiet line of relatives was waiting to see the man with the ledger sitting at the desk. And the smell was not of swimming pool chlorine and Bovril, it was of a thick, sweet disinfectant which made him want to be sick.

Reg had learned to swim here, and he could remember Shirley's rush to get in through those double doors to the white-tiled pool – NO RUNNING, NO PUSHING, NO BOMBING. And he was pleased today that he couldn't see through the crinkly, taped glass. He didn't want to go in. What he wanted – and *all* he wanted – was to know whether any hint of his daughter had been brought in from anywhere near to Flaxton Road.

The man was shiny. He had a shiny bald head, and a shiny face from a close shave, and his council suit with its coat of arms was rubbed shiny to a gleam. His voice was shiny, too, and his fingers slipped over the pages of his ledger as if they were oily fish.

'What was the name?' The smoothness of the voice was worse than if the man had shouted.

'Lewis – Reginald Lewis, that's me – but she wouldn't have her name on her.' He couldn't go on. He didn't dare to think what bits of her anyone might find after such a bomb. He came across victims every raid, but he didn't want to relate any of that to his Shirley.

'So what is it you want to know?'

'She wasn't found. After the bomb in Flaxton Road. She wasn't in the shelter . . .'

'Any other casualties?'

'Her mother, in a coma in St Nick's.'

'Have they dug anyone else out?'

'There wouldn't have been anyone else.' Reg suddenly lost his rag. 'I've been through all that with Civil Defence and Heavy Rescue. All I want to know from you is whether you've got any . . . unidentified remains . . . that could be a little girl.'

The mortuary manager looked up from his ledger. 'I haven't got a toenail without a tag on it, sir. We're right up to date today. Sorry.' And he closed the book, leaving a finger in it for the next inquiry.

Reg backed out of the baths and took a breath of London air – still thick with smoke from last night's raid, a choking fog of wood and magnesium and crude fuel from the oil bombs. But it was sweet to him. And he was glad that they hadn't found what was left of Shirley. Imagine her being seen over by that man in there . . .

The queue to go in backed up the street. People on their own, little family groups, a soldier on leave standing crying, two children clutching a gran – all waiting with those pale, pinched faces. And as he walked back up to St Nick's, he thought how, when Vera came out of her coma, he didn't want her doing it around here. She'd taken enough without becoming conscious in such a suffering part of London. And there was nothing here for them. No house any more, not even his daughter's grave to visit. He pushed his legs at the steep pavement, remembered the hill this had been for Shirley, felt the weight of her on his shoulders, giving her a flying angel after a swim. He closed his eyes, couldn't bear the pain of these memories. And from that feeling of wanting none of it any more, the idea came to him, before he got to the top of the hill. Vera had a sister in Cardiff. If he could get her down to Wales, he'd put straight in to his station officer for a transfer. They'd been marvellous to him over everything so far. He was still on duty only by choice, and Cardiff was being bombed. It wouldn't be cowardly to be transferred to another line of target docks . . .

Because with his last hopes of finding someone to bury just lost at the mortuary, Reg knew that the old life was over. They were going to have to start all over again; and do it somewhere else.

The yard of the country school had gone quiet. All Johnnie could hear was the chanting of multiplication tables. A stick was whacking the beat on a blackboard, and Johnnie's head went to it.

He could picture what else was happening inside the school. He could just see little Shirley in the headmaster's room while the police were being phoned. Him standing between her and the door. And the country police would easily know where the gypsies were camped. Johnnie hadn't come that far. So he could get off and find his receipt book without little Shirley to slow him down. Or he could do his best to stop her going back to mad Bren.

No choice. He had to face it out. He had to take himself into that school and tell them 'Plumstead', because he knew she wouldn't. He had to finish the job he'd started when he'd run her off.

The tables drill stopped and everything inside went quiet. From the field behind the school he could hear the jingle of harness and the rattle of stones as a horse ploughed. But from inside the building you could almost hear the scratch of the pen nibs. And his first idea of going straight in and facing up to Barney Bull had suddenly gone where dead birds went. Better have a look at the lie of the land, then, see some *other* person he could tell, perhaps some nice old lady teacher?

There was a wooden seat under a handy window. He'd have a look, anyhow. He hopped over the school wall and crept as careful as a bomb-disposal man across the yard; came to the seat and wanted to thank Mrs Mott on the brass plate for giving it, because he'd have a grandstand view into the hall from there.

School hall? There was no such thing in the country. Looking in through the bottom row of pink glass he saw just how small this school was. It wasn't a hall, it was the classroom, direct in from the porch. And there were all the kids, sitting in rows facing the blackboard and easel, heads up and down like dippy ducks, doing a board of sums. Pounds, shillings and pence, adding up. And facing them at the front was Barney Bull the teacher, drinking a cup of tea and dunking a biscuit, his fat backside on a cushion. He wiped his moustache and looked up at the children, and when he did the heads went down quick, not to catch his eye. Johnnie's too, just in case.

But there was no sign of Shirley. No office, no telephone, no little girl standing there saying 'Pip, Squeak and Wilfred' to anyone. No nothing. Johnnie risked it again, looked all round the classroom, from the younger ones near the front to the older ones near the back. He looked behind the teacher's chair to where there was a door, open just a bit. On it hung a raincoat and a trilby hat – and the cane, one of those 'My Best Friend' polished jobs with the tip of it done up with black cotton. And someone had had it that morning, because it was hooked on top of the raincoat. Through the slit of the door, though, Johnnie got a slice of something else. A smaller room, and just a chance the bit of moving about he could see was the Babies' class. Was that where Shirley was till the coppers came?

Johnnie came down off the seat and ran round to the back of the school. And if there *was* someone up in the sky, and he sort of thought there could be, there'd be a back door to this place.

He crept round the corner to where his prayer was answered. The door to the Babies', had to be. Creeping closer, he could hear the bits of chatter from inside – not the words, just the ups and downs. The door knob was big and brass and took a two-handed effort, even for him; but it turned, and it didn't wake the dead, and he could give himself a crack to see through into the room.

It was what he thought he'd see. The Babies' class. Near the door there was a clotheshorse hung over with painted bricks to make a little house, there were brown leaves in a jam-jar on the teacher's desk, and a row of crayoned sailing boats all along the pinning rail. With a teacher at the front looking as young as Biddy, only smart in a frock.

And there was Shirley. The teacher was bending down to her all kind, and Shirley was drinking a bottle of milk through a straw.

Just the ticket! Someone kind who reckoned even a little gypsy kid might like a drink. And with the being pleased, Johnnie had a sudden jealous feeling that Shirley wasn't far off being all right. Because he'd found who he'd wanted, someone he could give his message to. Not his nice old lady, but a kind young teacher – who could ask for more? Someone he could talk to without being scragged. He could tell her: 'Her name's Shirley, an' she ain't a gypsy, so don't give her back to them. She's from Plumstead in London and she's been stole from her mum and dad.' He could keep in the doorway for answering questions and still get away if Barney Bull came to get to him.

He looked at the sky and he looked at his feet. Shirley was safe. She wouldn't get a better chance, short of being delivered back to Plumstead in person.

Johnnie opened the door and went in, not too far. One or two of the kids stared at him, then carried on.

The others weren't bothered. The teacher stood up. Shirley stopped drinking. Johnnie opened his mouth.

When a bell rang. A change of lesson already? But it had come from further off, on the road – and wasn't that a loud grinding lorry racking up its handbrake? And suddenly it was Dukesey Joyce shouting, 'Lum*ber*, old lum*ber*, any old iron an' railings?' Just like Grandad Wally did.

Johnnie kept his voice level, didn't know how, it had to be one of God's miracles. 'You coming, kushti?' he asked Shirley. 'Get on with our door-knocking?' He tried to growl a bit like Christy would, even as he winked. 'Thank the nice lady for the cow juice.'

And he stood and waited, looking calm – the blood in him pounding his ears.

But what would Shirley do? Would she come, or would she want to stay – and then get caught, given back to the gypsies and mad Bren?

She was just staring at him, her skirt slipped down, needing a hitch.

Then good as gold, she handed the bottle of milk back to the teacher, and ran over to Johnnie.

'Thanks, Miss,' Johnnie said. 'You ever want anything sharpened . . .' And he backed them both out of the door – running them like the devil was chasing, across the back yard and into the field where the horse was ploughing, on down into the valley – before Dukesey could get a sight of them. And by some miracle they kept their feet.

So he'd been right. The gypsy hadn't been far

behind. And he knew it was more than scrap the man was after.

He pulled Shirley along, nearly had the arm out of her body; and in the panic of it she fell flat, winded herself, and started crying. He picked her up, got her going again, ignored the tears till they got to the trees. Under a shedding alder tree he wiped her smeared face on his scarf and put it back round his neck.

So what the heck was he up to? This was the last thing he should have been doing, forgetting to look after number one. He'd never get by, toting her along.

'Pip, Squeak an' Wilfred!' Shirley moaned, clutching into him as he rubbed at her knee.

'All better,' he said. 'Big girl! Come on, we got a jungle to get through 'ere. Find some other old road, eh, over the back?' He took her deeper into the trees, well out of sight of the school. 'That ain't the only road, you know.' *And find a shop or a pub and someone kind*, he told himself. Got to! Because he was dead certain now. He wouldn't stand a dog's chance till he got shot of her.

11

THE THING was, Reg had found, when you were grieving people avoided you: went the long way round or dived through some handy door if they saw you coming. After the bomb everyone had signed a black-edged card and put in to buy him a rub of Digger Plug tobacco. But after that it was as if they thought bumping into him was like walking under a ladder – bad luck. The boys in Blue Watch were OK – they all got flung about by the same kicking hose too often – but the rest of the fire station saw him coming and swallowed.

Station Officer Caesar, though, brought Reg into his office with a friendly grip. He sat him by the cold gas fire and offered his tobacco pouch. 'What can I do you for, Reg?'

Reg said no to the smoke and leant forward, arms on knees. 'Straight to it. It's a posting. I want to get the wife down to Cardiff, to her sister's . . .'

'The hospital says she can go?'

Reg blew out his cheeks. 'Might as well, seems to be the message. She still hasn't fluttered an eyelid, and without the key to get her wanting to come back . . . perhaps her sister's little girl can do what I can't . . . stir something up.'

Caesar stared him in the eyes. A straight man, he never held off a roasting or a hard fact. 'They're still talking about all that, then?'

'The hospital Sister was hopeful, but she thinks time's running out. Danger is, I'm going to lose her as well as –' He could hardly get her name out these days. Shirley's. 'She'll just slip off one night . . .'

'And you want a posting to stay near her?'

'That's the top and bottom of it.' Reg knew Bill Caesar wouldn't have the final say, that would have to come from District Control at New Cross; but he could put in a word. 'Cardiff's taking a heavy bombing. I won't be ducking out.'

'I'll put it up, Reg. Any idea when?'

Reg shrugged. 'As soon as. They need the bed.'

'Right.'

'There's only the war now, to keep us here.'

Bill Caesar looked him in the eyes. His own wife and children were safe in Worcester. 'Nothing, then? Nothing at all of the girlie?'

Reg looked to the threaded carpet to shake his head.

'Except in there, Reg.' He tapped his own forehead. 'She's always going to be in there.'

Both men blew their noses, together, like drill. And in an awkward shuffle in the small room, they got up and started patting for their pipes.

Shirley had had a bottle of milk and Johnnie had had nothing, but that was just tough luck, so he got them on, through the wood, to where there was a gate to another road.

'Come on, girl,' he said. 'Not far.'

He wasn't used to so much hedge and ditch all day, and his guts gave a little squirt of a thrill when they came to a few houses joined together. Another village – but bigger than that place with the church and the water tap. There were people about, a couple of parked cars, and a bus stop; and a general *built-up* feel that made him reckon he might be getting to the end of the country at last. His old London might not be a million miles away.

He kept a weather eye out for Dukesey's lorry, also for anything in khaki or police dark blue. But among this lot, he reckoned – little village green, pub, telephone box, petrol pump and shop – there had to be the person he was looking for. The trusty person. Shirley's ticket back to Plumstead.

''Old my 'and,' he told her, 'an' if you get asked a question, talk nice. Forget your old Pip, Squeak an' Wilfred an' let's have "Ello, goodbye, an' kiss my backside". Just behave yourself like you're someone they're gonna want to 'elp!'

He whistled as he walked, kicked at small stones as the road suddenly started having a pavement. He hadn't seen a pavement for two days. A bossy-looking woman in a hat came towards them with her shopping. But she walked right on past.

Johnnie went straight for the village shop. It was one of those places that sold everything: newspapers, heels, paraffin, cigarettes, knitting wool, toys, groceries – he could see it all through the criss-cross taping on the window. A sun blind was pulled down over

160

the pavement, a side flap saying ICE-CREAM – which had to be from before the war. Martins' General Stores. There was a little balcony over the shop front and a fancy porch above the door -- like the sort of shop you saw on a day down at the sea. But it had a real family look to it, like Old Mother Mogg's on the corner of Brick Lane, and he could just picture some-one like her serving inside. Sitting up on a stool on account of her legs and getting people to reach stuff down. Just the job for getting Shirley off his hands.

Except he'd need time to talk to her, wouldn't he? Give the line he'd had ready for the teacher. And he wouldn't have to be put off by customers coming in. The ideal would be two people serving, or an empty shop. One for the rest and one for him. Which sud-denly fitted. It had to be dinner-time closing, because as he was bossing in through the window, someone came to the door and started to turn round the OPEN and CLOSED card. A man in a grey shop jacket, worn over a long white apron. He looked up and down the street, making sure he wasn't missing a good paying customer.

Just one fly in the ointment. *Gypsy.* Johnnie looked the gypsy, and all that had got him up to now was a kicking from the school. He'd best not risk it again. He whipped off his scarf and stuffed it in a pocket. He licked his hands and flattened his hair.

''Ang on. Don' move! Be good, won' be a tick,' he told Shirley. And as the man finally turned his card, Johnnie pushed open the door and slid in.

Which was just like lobbing in a hand grenade, or

being Adolf Hitler himself. Never mind Johnnie not looking so much the gypsy, the man spun himself round like Punch and whacked at him, missed. He was short and heavy, his big moustache twitching like something with a life of its own. What Johnnie's dad called a real old Billy Bennett. And having missed, he was shouting the odds like the siren going off.

'Get out, how many times? Come here! Get out!' He didn't know whether to hold his door against the hordes or grab Johnnie by the scruff and boot him out. 'Can't you read – you London brats?'

Johnnie got only the quickest look at the shop's inside: old creaky floorboards and a carpet runner to tangle his feet in. He faced a few comics and books – thought about grabbing an annual to bat the man with. But Billy Bennett had seen it was only Shirley outside, not a trainload, and with his shop bell tinkling like the Toy Town police, he was holding the door open and giving out with hate.

'Get back to your slums! You ain't rationed with me.'

Johnnie got out past him, ducked the clump he thought was coming. Got a snotty snort and the slam of the shop door. And when he looked back to give the two fingers, he saw what he'd missed going in – the sign still swinging like a taunt in the face: NO EVACUEES WITHOUT AN ADULT.

'Come on!' he said to Shirley. 'Gotta sort ourselves out.'

And one of the things to sort was still Shirley. Her

still being with him, and him getting back to London, *and* being hungry – and the fact that right now, to be honest, she'd had it. She'd been toddling on her little legs since early morning, and now she'd run right out of steam. They had sleeps in school for kids like her, and she definitely wasn't going much further without a lie-down. He swore, inside. Why couldn't he have unloaded her?

He held her hand and had to keep his nerve as a bus drove up and stood shaking at the stop outside the shop. It sounded like Pricey's and it swung him round, quick, but it was a regular service, 144B, a green country bus. A woman got off and walked away up the road. Johnnie stood by the warm engine, and he sniffed in the traffic smell he was missing, out in the country. And he longed for the stink and the shouts of Aldgate. He went to the front where the radiator cap was doing its own little boiling dance. 'Alexandra Park', it said on the front destination blind. The buses had parks or pubs on them these days, so the Germans wouldn't know where they were if they landed.

But Johnnie did, didn't he? The name rang a loud bell. Alexandra Park, where his dad took him for the horseracing – when they went for a ride out on a bus; a lemonade and then back home wanting to wee all the way.

The bus took itself off. If he was right, that had him well on the right track. Follow the bus stops and get to Alexandra Park. He'd know where he was then and he could track back to Aldgate. He ground his teeth, chewed on it. Not much had gone right for him up to now, but wasn't this *something* . . .?

'You wanna little sleep?' he asked the girl. No answer. Well, no kids liked to sleep, but she really was done in. 'Come on, Johnnie find a kip.'

Not that he knew where. Woods were best, or a grassy slope in the sun. He'd follow the bus route, anyhow, see what little corner showed itself.

He walked them on through the big village, all dinner-time quiet, just the one main road to follow. But Shirley was getting slower by the step, and when they came to a big spreading tree with a seat around it, set plonk in the middle of the road, she sat herself down with the look on her that said she wasn't going another step. Not for anyone.

Johnnie made no bones about that. He knew when to make bones and when to play along – his dad was a past master at that. He sat down next to her. What he didn't want was to be taking too long about it, because out in full view like he was, anyone on the chase could drop on them as easy as a pigeon on a statue.

But was playing her along what he needed to do? Or was leaving her there more the ticket? If he'd nicked a pencil and pad out of that shop, he could have sat and written a note to tell anyone everything. And get off at his own speed, where the bus had gone.

But note or no note, Pricey could come along before anyone else; and Johnnie had only had to hear her screaming the once to know he'd never leave her to that. He wouldn't leave a dog to that.

Who could credit there wasn't someone he could leave her with? He'd had real rotten luck, at the village and the school and the shop. Three down in a row. Well, being superstitious, didn't the next time have to be a thumbs-up?

Shirley had started to close her eyes. They opened and closed in the sun, the openings getting a little bit narrower each time, like, his dad in an armchair with the *News of the World*. She'd be off in no time, and a right dead weight to carry.

''Ere,' he said, 'got somewhere proper for us to kip. Come on.' He gave her a gentle shake. He hadn't anywhere in mind, but he had to get them off the bull's-eye of the target, here in the middle of the road. Her little head was starting to loll. 'Johnnie's got a good idea. Coming?' He stood up. She hadn't said a lot to him today except 'Pip, Squeak and Wilfred', but she knew what he was saying to her all right. And she wasn't daft. If he went off she'd follow, or be left to all sorts of nasty things . . . She'd come toddling after him at the wishy-washy man's, hadn't she?

'Coming?'

He started to walk away up the road, listening; but when he heard nothing, he looked round under his arm. At first he thought he'd played it wrong, because she stayed. But a couple more steps and she slid off the seat, her skirt all hitched in the wooden slats. She freed it, and came running after. He took hold of her hand. 'Jus' round the next corner,' he said.

And, not believing his luck, what he saw made him right.

Round the bend the road took them on to a common, the usual sort – gorse bushes at the side and grass in the middle. But this one had an old pavilion at the far end and a pub down the other side: it was a wide and open common like a fair-sized corner of Wanstead Flats. The difference being, where Wanstead Flats was dug up with mounds and trenches to stop German gliders landing, this common was parked all over with old cars and vans, serving the same purpose. Johnnie took it all in, and whistled. They'd have had a bucketful of fun with these back in London, him and the boys! Old cars to play in, sitting up and see-sawing the steering wheels like racing drivers. Twisting the gear levers like joy-sticks for Battle of Britain dog fights over the river. Camps, gang hide-outs – and all wasted out here in the country.

Which was thinking like a kid who still played games. But think like a man on the run and what had he got? More than twenty places to doss down and lie low. Leather car seats to choose from for Shirley's sleep . . . No, son, this common of old vehicles wasn't wasted at all.

'There y'are,' he said. 'What you fancy? Straight Eight, Austin Ruby, Rolls-Canardly?' The choice of cars was nearly all black, but as they came to the first off the road, the possibilities were cut down in other ways. These had been got at already. Engine covers were loose, and what was inside was stripped of anything worth having. Standing on the running board of a Morris Ten, he could see there weren't going to be many with steering wheels left, let alone seats. And someone had done their toilet business in this first one. The flies and the smell had him off the running board in double-quick time.

He ran between the vehicles, snatched looks at the insides. Further over, there was an old-fashioned locked Bentley which hadn't been got at too badly. Probably not been there long. Shirley caught up with him as he looked in through a window. The inside looked real kushti, and a locked car door was nothing to a boy who'd been in *HMS Greengates*.

He looked through to the inside of the door on the opposite side, measured where the window winding handle was – how far down from the windowsill, how far along from the opening crack. He licked his finger and marked a similar place on the outside of the door he was standing at. He moved back, minded Shirley out of the way, and he went on going till he touched the car behind him. He waved the girl to keep standing still, and on a count of 'One, two, buckle my shoe!' he ran forward in line with his finger mark and gave the Bentley's door a flat hard kick where the handle was. The window shot down with a clunk, as good as gold.

'In we go!' He reached inside the car and found the door catch, opened it, and wound the window up again. Leaning over the seat – cosy warm leather in the sun – he helped Shirley in.

'There you go!' he told her. 'Fit for the Emperor of Abyssinia!' She scrambled up and sat with her legs straight and her gypsy-girl boots just coming to the edge of the seat. He sat next to her; and, wouldn't you know it, she was wide-awake now! Even with the glass and the sun and the dreamy smell of the old luxury upholstery, she was a million miles off going to sleep.

'Try an' 'ave a little rest,' he coaxed, 'then I'll get us some grub.' He was eyeing the pub, the Goat, saw a side door with a Bottle and Jug off-licence, where there'd be Smith's crisps and big Bath Oliver biscuits in a jar. Where a quick kid like him could steal something to eat while the man bent down for his lemonades. And for a moment he thought she'd at least try to shut her eyes.

Till she screamed.

She screamed as if she'd just been stung by a wasp. Sudden and loud and as tortured as any noise he'd heard come out of her since she'd first sat up in Bren's bed. It jumped him, jumbled his bones and muscles.

'What the . . .!' And he saw where she was staring. The terror shining out. Screaming and shaking over at where Johnnie had been looking just seconds before: at the Goat. Where Tommy Price was coming out of the public bar and looking round at the world with beery eyes. Johnnie pulled her down on the seat, but she screamed more than ever down there, getting fast into hysterics.

'Shut up! Be quiet! Darlin' . . .' He wanted to put his hand over her mouth, but he'd once seen a man do that to a woman in the street, and it only brought things on worse. Panic had to come out somewhere. 'He'll hear you! You want him to hear you?' Johnnie spared a quick look up over the seat.

Pricey was still outside the pub, but he was looking round like he was making up his mind which way to go. And, God help them, it was their way. He was turning about as if he was checking that no one was calling him back to buy him another, and then he crossed on to the grass of the common, heading towards them.

'Do stop your noise, for Gawd's sake! You want 'im to get you?' And even to Johnnie it was like the threat of Adolf Hitler. He looked again. Pricey was a way off yet, swaying between the cars as if he were proving how steadily he could still walk. But still coming on. Johnnie had seen him like that too often to want to be on the wrong end of that skinful of drink. Pricey was muttering the way he always did before someone copped it. And even though he had to go round and between cars, he was still on track to come past and hear Shirley and grab them.

And it was no good getting out and running. The man wouldn't catch Johnnie, but he'd have Shirley, sure as eggs.

'Shirley! Little girl! Gawd! Put a sock in it, can't you! He's coming!'

His own stomach was up eating his heart. So was it now? Was it now the time to go and leave her to her luck, if she was going to get caught anyway? Was Johnnie's best chance to shoot out of the car and get under one of the others? Or just run?

What? He felt like punching himself in the face. While Pricey got hold of her? The little girl was out of her mind just seeing him! Him reaching in the car and grabbing her would kill her!

But what else? How could he ever damp her down? He only had words, and what words would work in the no time he had?

And he suddenly knew. Knew a one-shot chance, anyhow. '"Pip, Squeak and Wilfred"!' he said. 'Shirley! You want "Pip, Squeak and Wilfred"?'

The note of her wail wavered, before it picked up and went on louder. And still Pricey came on, looking about him now and frowning, sort of sniffing, like someone wondering where a smell was coming from, except here it was a vague noise distracting him.

But out of Johnnie's head had come the flash of something he hadn't remembered till now – on account of him dodging an angry old shopkeeper at the time. Now that other thing came back – what had rung his bell in the shop, up on the counter with the comics and the books. What he'd thought of batting Billy Bennett with. The annual – 'Pip, Squeak and Wilfred', standing up face-on. He'd seen it – the penguin, the dog and the long-eared hare.

'Got the book, 'aven't I? I can *get* the book. The annual, what you have your stories from. Ol' "Pip, and Squeak and Wilfred". Eh? Only, you gotta shut up . . .'

She looked at him, and turned her terror down, just a notch.

'You keep quiet an' I'll read you it to go asleep . . .' She looked at him again, through all the wet of her fear. 'Get down, all quiet, an' 'e'll go past . . .'

He waited, and she went into sobs.

170

'I promise! Then ol' "Pip, Squeak an' Wilfred". Like your mum and dad reads you, bedtime. It's in that shop, an' I'll get it . . .'

And she stopped.

'Now you get down 'ere, an' we'll lie still, while 'e goes on 'ome.'

She racked her body again, the big sob – and for just a second she looked like she was going to start up once more.

' "Pip, Squeak an' Wilfred", Johnnie'll get it when they open. An' we'll 'ave all the stories. All your favourites.'

She stared at him again, and not so much rolled as flopped her little body off the seat and down on to the floor of the car.

Johnnie took a quick look up. Pricey had come a lot closer. Like the chaser in a terrible dream, they always come on quick . . . But her noise had stopped, just the sobbing now, and Pricey wasn't looking about him so much, more wobbling himself round a car bonnet. Johnnie dropped down on top of Shirley. Strained his back holding the weight off her, but tried to give himself the floppy look of nothing more than a pile of old rags.

'Oi!' It was Pricey, shouting. 'Oi! It's me! Here!'

Johnnie went cold. As cold and numb as death. Till he heard a hoot; and a shout from somewhere else. And not sure whether it was his tremble, or Shirley's, or a tremble running through the two of them welded together, he risked a quick pull up and a look – to see Pricey striding and stumbling across the common to the other side, where Dukesey Joyce's scrap lorry was pulled up. Now Johnnie could risk a longer stare; and he watched the soldier get pulled up into the cab by a big hand and flung like an old coat on to the cab seat.

'Look! There 'e goes! He's going, see? He's off, won't get Shirley and Johnnie now.' Johnnie had pulled the little girl up to give her proof of the going, the way his dad would always show him the blot of a dead spider to show he'd done for it. And while they watched, the scrap lorry started up with a blow-out of blue smoke, and drove down to the end of the common, where it reversed and headed back in the direction of the last village.

'Good girl. See? You done well.' She was sobbing again, and sucking her thumb. He sat on the seat and cuddled her. 'Give 'im 'alf an hour an' I'm gonna go and get you that book. Promise.' She looked up at him, big wet eyes. 'Ol' "Pip, Squeak an' Wilfred", eh?'

And he couldn't be sure, but round her thumb she seemed to give him the start of a little smile.

12

It had to be planned like a bank robbery. That angry shopkeeper was nobody's fool, and anyone wanting something he was sitting on was going to have to know how to get his fat backside off it. But from a little look in Shirley's eye Johnnie started to think it mightn't be as hard as all that – he just might have a partner in the job. All at once she seemed to have a bit of a glint about her, something he hadn't seen since that first night in the bus.

A girl called Daisy from down his street was the best little twister he knew. She had the sweet look on her face which said she could stand for an angel on a tombstone – but underneath she was a real tough little tyke. She'd always do just what the big boys asked. Like keeping a shopkeeper busy while they stole from the counter, taking a long time finding her money – then she'd put on an innocent little face when they legged it with something. And she'd buy nothing. Johnnie kidded himself he could see her in Shirley right now. There was just a bit of that sparky Daisy look on her.

Well, who said what sort of family Shirley had to come from? Villains had pretty little babies, didn't they? So after she'd had her rest, he'd get her looking less of the toerag and more of the bridesmaid and he'd send her into the shop when it was busy. Get her to go for something the bloke hadn't got, or what he might keep out at the back. Then he'd have the Pip, Squeak and Wilfred annual away under his coat, like magic.

But definitely not yet. The shop was shut for dinner, and she did need sprucing up by a little sleep.

Like a good old friend the sun started to help him out. It warmed through the windows and it softened the leather seats, pulled out the luxury smell. And with his arm round her it wasn't long before Shirley had gone; one moment sitting up, the next leaning her dead little weight on to him.

He looked down at her, as best he could. He'd never been a boy for a cuddle, so the warm little body and the smell of her hair was something new; and so was the leaning in on him, trusting him. And it was all right, he liked it. He knew if he could see his own face in a mirror it would be all tight and serious, like a kid holding someone's baby. But, so? He felt like a little dad to her right now, and dads could put up with looking like any old thing for their kids.

As he sat giving her a cuddle, her breathing went deeper and deeper, down to where it didn't sound or show at all. And into Johnnie's head came Biddy. It could have been the smell of the hair, or on account of Biddy was never far out of his head anyway, but in the warmth of the car he could feel the closeness of her face when she'd come into his tent; he could hear her husky voice talking to him, quiet. And he imagined her being there with him now, cuddling Shirley on the other side, like in a game of Mothers and Fathers. And he tasted that Biddy taste in his mouth from when she'd kissed him in the dream, and he felt a new sort of tingle over the sensitive bits of his skin. He closed his eyes and he pulled the little girl closer; and not asking for it to happen, but not fighting it either, he drifted off to sleep himself.

But there were no more dreams, just the body rest he needed.

It was the chill that brought him back again, the sun out in the west growing soft and red with its heat all gone, the only warmth in the car what came from Shirley.

And there was another thing about his dad: he always kept his promises. If he said Johnnie was going to get a clout, he'd get one. If he promised a stay-up, he'd get that too, never mind Auntie Pearl on the settee flicking at her cigarette. If threats and promises were made, then they were kept. So Johnnie knew he'd do what he'd promised to Shirley. If she shut up, he'd said, she'd get the annual. So get the annual she would, sure as eggs.

But she'd still have to help him, be his Daisy. She was still a part of the plan.

He woke her gently, tried to be like his dad on a lie-in day. He leant over and wound down the window on her side so that a fresh little breeze could blow in on her. At the same time he unstuck her from him, and he whispered in her ear.

'Shirley! Come on, girl, we're gonna do the business, get you your annual: ol' "Pip, Squeak an' Wilfred", eh?'

She was too far gone at first even to hear him. But after a little shiver in the chill, she fidgeted, and she ground her teeth, and when Johnnie said it again she started to come to. For a second he thought she was going to cry, coming out of her sleep, so he crooned her awake. He went on over and over with, 'Shirl, Shirl, little girl – ol' "Pip, Squeak an' Wilfred", eh?' And, full marks, she sat up like a good 'un.

After which he didn't mess about. He didn't keep talking over what she'd got to do, and he didn't sweat on whether or not she'd do it. He got on. He stood her up out of the car and he sorted her out – hitched her skirt higher, twisted it over and over the belt. And he rolled down her socks so it looked as if she did have a pair of legs, and then he took off her cardigan. Last of all he combed her hair with his fingers, and gave her a spit-wash on the cheeks. And all the time he was saying, 'We're gonna get that "Pip, Squeak an' Wilfred", eh?' And shutting the door on the car as if he were coming out of 54 Woodseer Street to go round to the shops, he led her off by the hand, telling her what to do.

'Ask 'im for paraffin, that's all. A pint – an' you 'ain't got a bottle. If 'e wants your money 'fore 'e goes out the back for it, take a long time looking, down your dress, up your knickers, all that. Then, you smile ever so sweet an' you say you forgot it, an' you walk out of the shop slow, not running 'cos you

176

'aven't taken nothing an' you 'aven't done nothing wrong. Right?'

But the real bank robbery bit was what came after. The getaway and the meeting up. Taking the book off the rack would be kid's stuff to Johnnie.

'An' I'll tell you where I'll be. This tree, round the back of this.' He'd walked her past the tree with the seat on purpose – the one in the middle of the road. 'You sit 'ere an' you wait for me, even if it's 'alf an hour.'

Shirley looked up at him, and he couldn't be too sure about her after all. She didn't have the same Daisy look on from before she'd gone to sleep. On the other hand, she wasn't the little zombie she'd been all day, either.

He walked her on to the shop. They'd slept a fair time, and the sun should have told him the Billy Bennett shopkeeper wouldn't be too far off closing. But people left their shopping late in the warm weather, kept their rations cooler in the shop cold store than in their food safes, so when Johnnie got them to the shop there was a decent little queue to keep the man busy.

So far, so good, just what they wanted.

'You go in an' get in the queue. I'll hang back, put a few people between us.' He smiled, whistled, pointed at something in the window as a woman went in. He'd taken off his neck rag but that wasn't a problem either way; he'd be in and out too quick. The real problem was just coming up. 'You can say it, can't you? *Paraffin. Pa-ra-ffin.*' He looked at her. All she'd said the whole day was 'Pip, Squeak and Wilfred' – the last thing he wanted her saying, when the book was where it shouldn't be any more. Just standing staring would be better than saying that after he'd nicked it.

Then she saw it for herself. Looking in through the door, there it was, stuck up, the bright yellow *Pip & Squeak Annual 1939*. Shirley's eyes opened wide and her mouth made a little 'O', and in a quick shock she looked all hopeful through into the shop as if her mum or dad might be standing there.

'Gonna get that for you, you're on a promise, long as you can say *paraffin* all right. Eh? *Paraffin?*'

And Shirley looked pathetically up at him and she said it. 'Pafarrin.' And her eyes kept going into the shop as if some miracle was about to happen. But she had come snapping to all right. Johnnie knew she'd do the Daisy for him.

He opened the door and sent her in, and she stood queueing up like a good 'un. Another woman went in just after her, tried a little race to be first. And then an old man, but apart from a straight face from one and a smile from the other, they didn't bother Shirley. Good little kid, she just stood there, waiting to ask her question and get her annual. And Johnnie looked through the door at the book again. It had to be like some teddy bear to her, he thought, or his old jack knife they'd taken off him at the Juvenile – a special thing you always had, your little touch of what made you *you*. You grew up fast when you lost it; and you went back to happy days when you found it again. He could see her staring up at it, hoped to heaven she wouldn't grab the annual herself, and he thought about the night-time stories she must have had with her mum. And he knew if it were him he'd be ready to cry his eyes out; because he missed the old days just the same. He *had* to get her sent back home where she belonged.

Taking his time, Johnnie went into the shop himself and stood at the back of the queue. He took a deep breath to steady himself. He wasn't a thief. He didn't do this sort of thing down Brick Lane or up Commercial Street, but he did know what he was about. Aldgate boys always did.

The shopkeeper looked up as the door went and someone else came in after, but he didn't see Johnnie. A couple more people, and Shirley would be next, to send the man out the back for paraffin where it had to be kept for safety reasons.

Which was when Johnnie heard those same old words, but out of a different mouth.

'Those annuals you've got there, like that *Pip & Squeak*, are they reduced?' It was a tall woman with a fox fur round her neck, its little black eyes staring down at her feet.

'Reduced?' Billy Bennett looked back along the shop to the book.

'They're last Christmas, nearly a year old . . .'

'The latest edition, all the same, Mrs Freelove. Still –' He had Johnnie's dad's look on his face which said a sale was a sale. He was going to come and get Pip, Squeak and Wilfred. Johnnie couldn't believe his rotten luck.

'There's not a lot of reading about for the children
...' And the woman reckoned she was on to a bargain.

Not reckoning on Johnnie. Without thinking about
it he turned round, knocked down a rack of comics
and grabbed the book – and bolted out like a smash
and grab. Not hidden under his coat – it hadn't been
done all clever – but held tight in his hand as if he
were someone starving, with a bit of grabbed grub to
feed the kids.

The shop took a shock wave. Like that fraction
before a bomb blast, they all stood struck; then they
fell over themselves with shouts.

'Evacuee!'

'Little thief!'

'London kid!'

But Johnnie was quick. He could run behind tail-
boards and dodge horses and carts all day. He took off
as if Billy Bennett was burning his tail with a blow-
torch – down the village street and up the first dusty
alley on his left. Between two high fences, tight
mouth, shaking cheeks, till he came to a posh brick
house set back from everywhere else. Without looking
round, he climbed over its wall and dropped on to a
lawn, where he threw himself under a laurel bush in
the border. And he lay there as still as one of the garden statues he could see through the leaves; as still as
the thump of his chest would let him.

And no one came out; he hadn't been seen from a
window; so he stayed. Most people get caught in hide-
and-seek because they always try for a better place.

But what Johnnie knew was to stick with what you'd got. Get there and lie still.

A long way off he heard Billy Bennett's loud voice, but what he dreaded most, the crunch of footsteps coming down the alley to the house, he didn't hear. And he was patient. The book was under him and one of its edges stuck into a rib, but he bore it; and he bore it a lot longer than most could have done.

At the shop, Billy Bennett had run into the street, when his customers had stayed where they were: a place in the queue was a place in the queue. And no one took much notice of a little girl slipping out of the shop. After their first shouts they just shuffled up to close her place. Outside, the shopkeeper went right where Shirley went left and failed to see her as he looked round the first corner. He gave up, but he must have remembered her from the boy. When he saw the two women on the far side of the street, he shouted his abuse across at them.

'Thieving blighters! Oughta be locked up, evacuees, gypsies, the lot of you!' He threw his words like sticky mud as the women sorted a basket of firewood and pegs at their feet. One of them bothered with looking up. 'All tarred with the same brush, training your brats to do your thieving for you!'

Granny Joyce stood up tall from the basket and came over, the face on her that always gave the younger women a fright. She came up close to Billy Bennett and she chucked her head in a question.

He wasn't so sure now. 'Not your lot today, but you saw 'em – toerag about twelve, and a little baggage!'

'Two of 'em?' she asked. 'Big boy and little girl?'

Billy Bennett turned his back on her to show his disgust. Which was when another customer went into his shop, and he had to get back in case anything went missing in the way of rationed goods.

In the posh garden Johnnie Stubbs gave it a good fifteen minutes, and by the time he came back to the village street the pavement was clear on both sides. No sign of Shirley, no more than there was of anyone else.

Another bus went by, kicking up its dust on the London road, and Johnnie ran along in its trail to the meeting place; his mind going over and over the chances. Had Billy Bennett got her? Was she being grilled in his back room or in the nick somewhere? Or had she toddled off, got lost in the lanes?

With the thick book under his jacket, he ran for the meeting tree. The dust settled on the road and he spat in the gutter to clear his dry mouth. And at the approach to the tree, just under its spread of leaves, he stopped his running, and stood still. *London*, he thought. Woodseer Street and the duplicate books. The receipts that would say his hands were clean over the gold watch. The bus route which would take him nearer there.

He hadn't been chasing that proof like he'd planned. He hadn't even been thinking about it. It was Shirley he was worried over.

And it was Shirley who was sitting like a good 'un round the other side of the tree, her little legs dangling off the circular seat like a dolly on a shelf.

'Little darlin'!'

Her face tipped up, she slipped off the seat and took his hand. Without a word he walked her back to their car.

And they both knew the first thing they'd do when they got there. Like him and his dad getting back to their house – one putting the kettle on, the other sorting the bags – nothing needing to be said. Johnnie and Shirley got in the car and sat up on the back seat, and he opened the annual and found a story to read. No excuses, just promises kept.

Shirley waited patiently for whatever story he wanted to read to her. In went her thumb, and she waited, watching him: while Johnnie thumbed through the pages. He found a 'Pip, Squeak and Wilfred' story about donkey rides on the beach and Auntie Penguin getting her come-uppance. A favourite, sure as eggs. She listened while he made up his own words to the pictures, the way his dad did; and she didn't interrupt. Just leant on him like he was a chair arm, the thumb still in her mouth; and with her other hand she was reaching round the back of Johnnie's neck, twiddling the hair at the back of his head. It was a good feeling. He liked it, didn't want her to take her hand away – and Johnnie hung the finish out for as long as he could, before he closed the book. His dad's old rule had been one story if he was lucky and that was it. How would Shirley take that – because he was going to have to get food for their bellies? But she took it as good as gold. She held the annual for a cuddle, and reached herself up to Johnnie's face and she kissed him on the cheek. Hot and dry.

'Night-night, sleep tight,' she said, and she closed her eyes.

The light had almost gone, the blue print of that page in the book could have been black or brown. The air was still, no sirens went, the country was quiet. Dear little cock, Johnnie thought, treat her right and she's no bother at all. Like him – and like Biddy and her people, too. *Give as good as you get, and get as good as you give.* That's what his dad always said.

And now he had to get food; but not quite yet, not for an hour. He'd give Shirley an hour before he woke her up. Then it was food, get through the night, and be up real early to follow the bus route to London.

Dukesey Joyce's lorry was wearing a rut down the lanes between the gypsy site and Johnnie's common of cars outside the village. It had gone back once with Pricey and a load of scrap, returned to pick up the women out calling, and then come back to drop the soldier off.

'Shift as best you can,' Dukesey said. 'I'll be back when we've set us snares. You get them two runaways. You walk 'em down this road till I see you.'

Pricey slammed the door, said something to himself.

'They been seen here, the pair of 'em. They ain't gone far.'

'No, nor me. Not far enough. I'll be shot by the Home Guard for a German paratrooper, skulking round.'

'Gah! Pitchforks don't fire bullets.' Dukesey tried to put the lorry into reverse, but it wouldn't have it, so he drove it on the long way round the common.

The Goat, which the gypsy passed without a second look, was a London pub out in the country. But there wasn't a Bottle and Jug shop counter like Johnnie expected; this had something called the Country Bar. People came at it from the common. Country or not, all pubs had crinkly glass to stop kids in the off-licence shop from seeing the secrets of the pub, but nowadays they had the black-out, too, double drapes over the doors. This shop-lifting was hard to plan to the point Johnnie wanted. Down at the Seven Stars in Brick Lane he knew the lie of the land, just where the arrowroot biscuits stood, and the big box of crisps, and the side-on stacks of wooden crates with the beer bottles facing. But that worry went as he crossed to the door. The casky smell of barrelled beer came off the place, and it took him direct to Woodseer Street and the brewery wall facing his front room. He could almost hear the sound of hard and heavy drayhorse hooves on the road, and it made him see red again for the way he'd been treated – driven to this by being sold for a thief to *HMS Greengates*. He was going straight in here to take his chances. Wasn't he *owed* a stinking bite to eat?

'Get down the road, down there, about by that lamppost.' It was far enough away for Shirley not to be caught up in things. And he could run off first in the other direction and take the long way round the common and come back to her. She *would* come, wouldn't be left in the car. 'Yeah? See that lamppost?'

Shirley looked down the road. 'Bus stop,' she said.

'Yeah.' Now he could see the little sign. Good eyes, some kids had. Alongside the pathway there were cottages set back behind long gardens, all blacked-out and well shut off. She shouldn't be bothered by anyone.

'I'll see you down there, with some grub.'

Shirley clutched her annual tight to her jumper, as if it were a hot-water bottle in the night.

'See you as soon as soon.' She stood there for a moment. 'Go on.' And off she trotted.

In the distance he heard the clatter of another 144B, pulling away from the bus stop by Billy Bennett's shop; the route to follow to Alexandra Park. But all that could wait. He was going in this pub shop for grub. He pulled down on the brass latch, saw the sign he saw everywhere – NO GYPSIES – and he pushed himself in. Straight off, he put on the busy look of a boy with a message.

And who was that leaning on the bar, looking out at nothing as usual, and downing a pint like a pig? In his big old coat and the ugly face he didn't shave any more? Pricey! Uncle Tommy Price!

Johnnie didn't stop to look properly at all. He was turning round and getting out as if he were still coming in – fighting the black-out curtain and losing the latch – then out on the pathway to run Pricey off in the wrong direction.

Except he didn't. Because while he could still hear

Pricey taking a punch at the black-out, he also heard the bus coming round the common and bouncing along towards the next bus stop. Where Shirley was. And with the start he'd got on the man, Johnnie took a wild chance and chased the bus instead, which was slowing at a little girl on her own. As the platform came level to the bus stop he scooped her up onto it, and was grabbed for safety by the bus conductress. He shouted at her in a panic.

'Ring the Aunt Nell! Get off! He's a loony after us!'

And because the 'clippie' was from a London bus garage, she jumped to the ring of the rhyming slang for bell, and gave it the emergency three. Which had the driver pulling away like at a Grand Prix.

Pricey ran hard to catch them up – shouting his filth and grabbing out. 'Come 'ere, you little basket – or I'll 'ave you back in the approved!'

But he was never going to make it, thank God. Especially when the clippie rang her bell again to get them sailing past the next stop, the last before they got on the London road.

There was just time for Johnnie to shout back: 'Save your legs, Pricey – I'm sortin' all that!' And he timed the raising of two fingers to be sure the man was looking up to see it, then he grabbed Shirley on to a seat and started explaining himself.

13

'EVACUEES,' he told her, 'doin' a run. Smacked 'er an' belted me. Goin' back to our mum.' It was a true sort of thing to say. He'd heard it out totting with his grandad round Plumstead, seen it in the shop here. Some evacuees got very badly treated. The world was filled with people who didn't like others too much if they didn't come out of the same drawer.

The clippie in her navy-blue slacks, big earrings, made-up as smooth as a film star, gave a kind smile to Shirley, who sat up on a seat, clutching her annual. Then the woman looked at them hard, and 'Where you getting to?' she asked, the smile suddenly gone off her face.

'Alexandra Park. Ally Pally. Then through to the Tower 'o London.'

'Ain't got no money for fares, though, I bet.'

Too right, they hadn't. Johnnie hadn't held a copper coin in his hand for a week. He thumbed out of the back of the bus. 'Took all that for his beer, what our mum give us.' He gave her his best suffering look, the sort to get you off the cane at school. So which way was she really going to jump? She could cane them hard, put them off at a cop shop if she wanted.

She went on staring at them, then she winked, and

pulled two white *half* tickets from the ticket rack in her hand and with a little *ding* each she clipped holes in them.

'Two to Ally Pally. Now, how you gonna get on home from there?'

She was all right; she was good as gold. 'Get the other bus. Forty-two to the Tower,' Johnnie told her.

'That's about it.' She shook her leather pouch of money up flat and threw a catch of coins on to her hand. Picked out some of the silver stuff, what Johnnie's dad called shrapnel. 'Here y'are,' she said, 'an' don't tell a soul where you got it.' She looked down the bus. There was only one other passenger, a soldier asleep on the back seat, but her kindness was dead safe with Johnnie: he wouldn't give her away.

Now she sat herself in next to Shirley. 'What you got there?' She looked at the annual, but she wasn't into it really, more wanted to talk. 'They can be horrible, some of them country people. Don't get the bombs, but blame us for upsetting their apple carts.' She squinted out of a window and rang her driver on again, poking the bell with her ticket rack. 'Vicky-verky, there's some as nice as pie, can't do enough for you . . .'

There was a crossroads ahead, and the bus turned on to a major road, stopping soon in a little lay-by with a bus shelter. The clippie stood up to show willing in case there was a bus inspector about; but the only person getting on was an old man with a Scottie dog. She took his fare and came back to Johnnie.

'I got a boy, 'bout your age. He's down Dorset with

his auntie.' She lit another cigarette, a Weight from a little paper packet, Auntie Pearl's favourite smoke. 'Miss the little beggar – but at least I know he's safe ...'

Johnnie nodded, tried to look tired. He didn't want to get drawn in too much, telling lies about the mum him and Shirley were supposed to have, and where they lived. Besides, he wanted to think. This clippie was a kind woman. Believed him. *Trusty*. So had he found his 'out' for Shirley?

''Ad your tea before you run?' The clippie looked at Johnnie's pockets – with a twist of her red mouth to say he hadn't planned this very well, otherwise.

'No – took our chance, on the quick.'

'Did you?' She went back down the bus, handed off the old man and his dog on to a white-kerbed pavement where the road was thickening up with houses. They were getting closer into London. A few more got on now and she had a joke or two, and – 'Hold very tight please!' – dinged on the bell.

Johnnie moved Shirley in closer to the window. She was sitting up on the seat like a good little girl, and playing his game nicely. He couldn't do anything else but put his arm round her. And straight off, she snuggled into him, still holding her 'Pip, Squeak and Wilfred' tight in both arms. But a long way off sleep. She'd had two good snoozes in the day and even the throb of the bus wasn't going to send her off. Instead, she looked up out of her window, through the little rings in the sticky safety webbing.

'Happy birthday, moon,' she said out of nowhere,

with her first real smile since Johnnie had seen her. 'Do you like the moon?' she asked him.

'Oh, yeah. I love it.' He twisted his neck to see it, rising bright enough to make shadows. It was on the way out but not far off still being full – and he guessed those bombers would be over again tonight.

'Do you like the sky?' She was on a bit of a roll.

'Yeah, very fond.' Having a chat, finding things to say. He helped her. 'An' the 'ouses, an' the chimbleys, an' the trees, an all that. Can't get enough of 'em.'

She snuggled in closer. 'I like you,' she said. But it was very matter-of-fact, not sticky, and meaning all the more for that.

He gave her a squeeze.

'Here y'are, don't say I ain't done my bit for the cockney brigade!' And on to Johnnie's lap the clippie put a greaseproof-paper packet of sandwiches.

'Sarnies. Hope you like fish paste. Won't be what you've had down the country . . .'

'Ta! Thanks –' Not often was Johnnie left trying to sort the right words; and to be honest, instead of bothering, he was ripping the paper off. These'd hit the spot. While he had his think.

'See you on your way, won' they? Tell your mum it was given you by some other little evacuees's mum – a bit better billeted than you was . . .' She didn't say it loud, wasn't wanting to be heard doing the Good Samaritan. And to save Johnnie going red, she went off quickly down the bus.

He tucked in – and Shirley, bless her, waited to be offered. 'Bit o' tea,' he said – although little kids were funny, because hungry as she was, she still left her crusts behind.

And as Johnnie chewed, he thought hard about her, and the clippie, who was sitting down the front rattling the change in her pouch, staring out of the window.

He'd definitely found his trusted woman, hadn't he? This clippie was who he'd been looking for since first thing that morning. Kind, not daft, and in a bus going back to London. Smack right for doing what he wanted done. She'd given him money, bus tickets, her own supper. And he wouldn't have to put up his hands to being a liar; he could just tell her his story was all true – except Shirley wasn't his sister. And he wanted her put back to the police in Plumstead, where she came from.

He looked down at the little girl, picking crumbs off the top edge of her annual. She could talk again now, could probably say her address. He could ask her, and even if she was shy with the woman, *he* could say what it was.

Sweet as honey! He could leave Shirley at Ally Pally with the clippie and do what he had to at Woodseer Street. His plan was falling into place neat as an easy jigsaw.

'Your name's Johnnie.' It was Shirley telling him. Funny how little kids told you what you knew, like it was news.

'S'right,' he said. 'What's yours?'

'You know.' She put on a coy face, as if he were playing a game with her. 'Shirley.'

'Yeah, I know, don' I?' He gave it a couple of breaths. 'Shirley what?'

'Shirley-May-Lewis.' She said it quickly, all run in together, but still coming out special, like someone pulling out a string of pearls.

'Pretty.' He looked up at the clippie, who was standing now, looking out of the front of the bus through the square in the driver's blind. 'An' where d'you live?'

'Plumstead, London!' She said it like the surprise part of a game, the sort of word where you all fall down.

'An' what road? You live in a little road?'

Shirley shrugged her small shoulders. 'Shirley-May-Lewis. Plumstead, London.'

Which he reckoned was as close as he was going to get, but good enough, all right. And Johnnie was looking at the clippie with his heart thumping harder than ever it had in all his fights and escapes. He'd got it! He'd got the ticket for getting the little girl back. He really was like a dad now, because he could make everything all right for her. He only had to call the clippie down.

She'd turned from the driver's window, gave him a wink – and pulled her pencil out from her buttonhole to start making up her fare sheet.

'Johnnie. Story,' Shirley said. 'Pip, Squeak and Wilfred.' She shuffled her bottom the way birds feather down into their nest. And she gave Johnnie the annual to choose a story, her hand already up round the back of his neck. But he didn't choose. The book

193

fell open at a page printed in brown and he'd go with that because his mind was somewhere else.

The clippie came back down the bus, taking her time at each seat. They were getting near the end of the run to Alexandra Park. Her shift was nearly over. She swung in closer to Johnnie and Shirley. 'Having a story?'

And now was the moment. They were all alone, the three of them, and Johnnie could tell the woman anything he wanted, quietly. Shirley would be sorted in seconds.

'"Pip Swallows a Whistle and Wilfred Squeaks!"' he said, and as Shirley's thumb went in her mouth and she started twiddling his hair, he began the story – and let the clippie go.

Because for some reason, he wasn't having it. He wasn't trusting anyone with Shirley. He was going to do his receipt-book business at his house, then he was delivering her to the front door of Plumstead nick himself.

That's what a real dad would do.

Half a mile from the police station in Plumstead High Street, St Nick's Hospital had had one of its worst days. High-explosive bombs from Heinkel IIIs had hit two public shelters, one in the grounds of a vicarage and one in the Granada Cinema car-park. And a string of thirteen bombs had been let go by a lone daylight bomber, falling along a line of back gardens in Ann Street; all with Anderson shelters where people were packed. Scores of severe casualties were taken to the hospital, which was already run ragged by several nights of a raiders' moon.

But the Sister on Vera's ward still found time for a smile at Reg. Except, 'I wish I thought you were doing the right thing,' she told him. Reg had just come in, hadn't even sat down to hold the still hand on the blanket, and the Sister was passing through in a hurry with something she didn't want seen under a towel. 'She's been terrible restless. She's not for a move.'

'What do you mean?' It was all fixed up. One more night, then an ambulance to Paddington the next afternoon, and a berth on the hospital train to the west of England and Wales. His posting to a Cardiff fire station sat in his pocket. 'I've got to go now, it's signed and sealed.'

'Then unsign and unseal it. She's been all over the cot, twisting and turning. Don't ask me, but it's all in here. She knows.' The Sister waved the lumpy towel at her own forehead. 'I tell you, she won't take moving away from her daughter . . .' It seemed like the Sister wanted to get on, but she couldn't. Because she reckoned she knew, better than the doctors. 'You won't be moving her, I tell you – you'll be losing her if you do, you're . . . walking her away from her little one.'

'But I've got to. We've both got to walk away from her. We haven't *got* a little one. We've lost her, she's gone.'

'This one'll think you're giving up.'

Reg didn't shrug, he just looked.

'She'll *know* you're giving up.' The Sister shifted

the weight of the towel in her arms. 'You just keep on coming in. You keep up with your talk. She knows more of what's going on than you reckon. And I just happen to think it's near, her going one way or the other. I know that twisting and turning . . .'

Reg looked at his wife's face, the face of peaceful sleep; and he looked at this friend. 'You've been very kind, Sister. But we're going tomorrow.'

The Sister shook her head; but sadly, like losing a patient.

'Then Our Lady bless you,' she said. 'I'll pray for you. But don't come back to tell me when it's too late . . .'

Woodseer Street was a weird place at night. Facing the wall of the brewery, what you heard when it was dark was the odd clop of a big dray horse hoof in the yard, or the snorty blow of a nose in a haybag, or, best of all, the Niagara Falls of a shire horse splashing the ground with a foot-long pee. It was different tonight, though. When the blitz started the brewery horses had been evacuated to the country. And tonight the street was weird for Johnnie's own reason – it being where Johnnie lived, but didn't live. As he came at it from the Brick Lane end he took that first scared look every East Ender did, coming home. Was it all still standing there?

It was. His dad's second-hand shop on the corner was boarded up, but all present and correct. And their house a few doors down was still there in line with all the others. Further down looked a different part of

London, though. Something had hit the old rope warehouse and where they'd used to run past and chuck horse manure through the door at the moany sweeper, now there was all sky.

And he had Shirley with him. He'd kept her. He was going to do that giving her over bit himself. *So far, so good – so far*, like his dad said. But it wasn't till he got back to the blitz that what he'd done came up and hit Johnnie. If he lost Shirley now, or they got killed, you could lay it all at his door.

Her little hand had got tighter in his as they'd come up off the wider roads. He felt like he was leading her into a secret world of his own, bringing her into the quiet of Woodseer Street.

'All right?' he said. 'Not far.'

It was all blacked out, and there'd been no one much on the streets. The usual noise in the Seven Stars and he'd heard the nine o'clock pips on someone's wireless. But aside from that it was quiet, which was weird for this part of London. The war had to be getting to them. He'd steered Shirley past the Air Raid Wardens' post, with all its sandbags at the door, and he'd stood her in a shop front when a policeman came past on his bike. He'd led her round a bomb crater, and he'd put as much air space as he could between them and the public shelter with its white 'S' shining. But the air raid siren hadn't gone yet, and people were probably having their last cups of tea before going down. Then there'd be a bit of argy-bargy. Like one old pair who always stood on the pavement when the German planes came over, on account of they thought they could dodge what was coming down. Even old Harry Hewson, the air-raid warden, forever on about *Put that light out!*, couldn't push that old pair inside.

Johnnie came along the paving stones between his dad's shop and their house. He knew every one of the cracks. There were even some of his chalk marks still about, an old game of noughts and crosses. A motor-bike without a tarpaulin leant outside number 50 where Daisy's mum lived. It gave off a hot smell – some sailor on leave called in for a kiss, sure as eggs.

And here was home, number 54. Johnnie stood back across the road, looked up at the state of it. Slates off the roof – and the attic window busted, with a bit of curtain hanging out. Not too bad, given all the bombing. Otherwise it looked the same as when his dad went marching off, all locked up. Now to give that window lock a seeing-to. That, or he'd go for a small pane in the front door – what was a little bit of broken glass against getting his proof about the watch? He could hear what his dad would have said: 'You're clean as a whistle, old son! *Break down a hundred doors!*'

Johnnie's heart started going again, getting this close to what he wanted. Coming this near to telling 'Captain' Rosewarn he could kiss his bum!

'See? Where Johnnie lives.'

Shirley looked up at the house, showed interest – but one hand still gripped tight for him and the other for 'Pip, Squeak and Wilfred'. He led her forward across the road.

'Open,' she said.

'Yeah, what I'm gonna do . . .'

'Open!' She nodded her head at the front door. And now Johnnie saw; it *was* open, just a crack. He wasn't going to have to break any glass. That bomb down the road had done it for him, blast-busted the lock.

He stood still on the pavement, suddenly didn't feel so brave. An empty house is an empty house, even your own. Shirley stood there like a good 'un, waiting while he found his guts. Because it was no good him looking for someone to go in with them. He wouldn't know where to start, finding a mate to hold his stupid hand. If only Biddy could have been there. And that just gave him the courage. No hanging about then! He'd push into that house like his dad would, scared of nothing. Cock of the heap.

He took a step, and in a sudden ghostly wail the air raid siren started up. That growl, that scary start, then up and turning your stomach over. Joined by the next one over Aldgate East. And Shirley knew about sirens. She pulled him to the front door, and he went with her. From the corner of Woodseer Street and Spital Street he could hear old Air Raid Warden Hewson shouting, 'There's your siren. Put that flaming light out!'

Johnnie pushed the door. No letters on the mat, but no horrible little telegram: the army sent a telegram when a soldier was killed. He brought Shirley in and he pushed the door shut, pulled the black-out across it and tried the light: the *electric* light, as his dad still called it. And it came on. It worked. Could be from when the police had been in.

He stood inside and looked round at the hall, and up the stairs – and if Shirley hadn't been holding on to his hand he would have stood there and cried. Johnnie Stubbs was home. His dad wasn't; he'd gone marching off; but this was Johnnie's home, too, and he was in it again. And it hadn't changed, not old 54 Woodseer Street. There was a damp, chilly, shut-up feel about the place, but the wallpaper was the same old pattern, and the stair carpet was worn in the same places, and the monks fishing in the picture on the wall still hadn't caught a kipper. And on the hallstand his dad's Sunday cap still hung on the end of his billiard cue.

'Johnnie's 'ouse,' he said.

But what else was that? The smell of burning, not wood but a back-yard smell of burning rubbish, coming from the front room. Sniffing, Johnnie led the way and went in, put on the light as he pushed the door.

To see Pricey in his long coat sitting there in the armchair, a fag on and warming his boots at the fire in the grate. Smiling, just swivelling his eyes to see that the black-out was up at the window.

Johnnie was half-way out again, quick. Stopped dead by what Pricey said. 'Don' be stupid all yer life! If I don' grab you I can grab 'er, an' she's the one I'm 'ere for!' He didn't bother with moving a muscle.

Johnnie stood stock-still, Shirley holding him there with a grip like one of those dogs that never lets go. But she didn't scream. She clutched her annual so tight she dented an edge, and she wet herself.

Pricey crossed and uncrossed his ankles, and slung

on to the fire what he'd been burning to take the chill off the room: an old picture frame and the tight screwed pages and the covers he'd torn from the duplicate books out of the cupboard.

Receipt books! Johnnie's proof! Gone up the chimney in smoke!

'You . . . big . . . scuddin' . . . turd!' Johnnie could hardly say it for the choke.

'Little game's up, i'n't it, son? Too cocky by 'alf, weren't you?'

Johnnie didn't feel a thing any more, just Shirley's tight little hand.

'But what we'll do, we'll get back down the country on the motor-bike, an' that'll be the end of it . . .' So that was how he'd beaten the buses here. Stolen that AJS.

'Listen, you got a mate in Dukesey, so you ain't got no problem with him. You come back – or I do worse to the both of you, an' they dig you up where the next bomb hits.'

He still hadn't moved out of the chair, and his look said he didn't have to: he really was cock of the heap. And all Johnnie could do was stand and listen to it, with that boiling in the gut that scalds, the blistering you get when people cane you, that rotting inside that won't get better if you live to be a hundred.

And the man was in his dad's best chair, alongside his dad's little cupboard of trade prices and the one pen that worked, and what had been his two or three duplicate books – leaning his greasy head where his dad's hair should have rested, him who was away fighting.

Up above, the air raid was on, that drone of engines. And as they stood, him and Shirley, a whistling came, and a bomb fell somewhere this side of the river.

'We got a shelter,' Johnnie said. Any chance.

'Stuff shelters! We're here till the all-clear.' No argument about it. Pricey took in a great lungful of his cigarette.

From along the street came the shout of old Hewson telling someone over the brewery wall where he reckoned the last one had hit.

'Man!' said Shirley, hearing the voice.

And without the first idea he was going to do it, Johnnie was out of Shirley's grip and across that room, pulling the black-out down from the window in one great yank.

Pricey was up, like from an electric chair. He half went for the curtain, then for the light switch. But Johnnie was going to die defending that, he had to keep the law-breaking light on, he had to bring Hewson in. He held a dining chair up at Pricey like a lion-tamer, poking, prodding. Pricey came in over the top of it and grabbed at Johnnie's hair, getting hold and bashing him on to the chair leg and against the wall. But still Johnnie held on.

'Put that light out! They're overhead! Bombers up there. What's your ruddy game?' Old Hewson was at the window looking in.

Seeing Johnnie ramming the chair into Pricey's gut. But his coat took most of it, and he started booting Johnnie up in the air, one on the knee, one on the

202

thick of his thigh. Shirley was elbowed back against a wall, standing there screaming. Another kick, where it hurt the most, and Johnnie was doubled over, wanting to be sick. But he wasn't giving in. Somehow he forced himself up to stay between the man and the light switch.

'What the deuce is going on? *Put that light out!*' Old Hewson was coming in at the front door, up the passage. Pricey had got hold of Johnnie's neck, was going for the kill. But Johnnie had time to spit in his face and Pricey let go, to suddenly turn instead to try a grab at the light flex dangling in the middle of the ceiling – and missing.

Hewson fell over Johnnie as he pushed into the room.

'Johnnie Stubbs! This ain't your dad!'

Too right it wasn't! His dad didn't fight kids, he was off fighting Germans.

Shirley was still screaming her head off when another bomb blasted earth and slate and glass through the air: a little girl's shrieking which brought a policeman running from Brick Lane. Light shone out across the pavement, throwing fighting shadows on the brewery wall.

'Tommy Price!' Johnnie shouted at the law as it came in and whacked off the light. 'You're after him! Royal Artillery. Army deserter. You ask!' And as the policeman came in and threw Pricey to the floor, Johnnie ran Shirley into the hall.

He swivelled on the pavement. Which way to run? With just the last words of the soldier following after them as it went quiet when he was sat on.

'An' you, *Johnnie Stubbs! They'll 'ave you, I'll see to that –'ere, Plumstead, wherever . . .!'*

But Johnnie wasn't listening. He was off running up the street. He'd still got Shirley and by some miracle she'd still got her annual. He ran her up Woodseer Street, down Brick Lane, round another corner and dodged them into a public shelter. They'd be well lost in the crowd in there. They could draw breath, and he could dry his girl out somehow, and nurse his head and private parts. Wait for the morning, and go out with the workers.

But one thing was hurting which he couldn't rub away. His dad's receipt books had gone up in smoke. And along with them his chance of proving that the gold watch was his, all legal.

14

IN THE stuffy, smelly public shelter Johnnie made up his mind. It wasn't one of those friendly shelters – all singing and joking and loads of luv-a-duck – but a place where no one would give an inch of their space, and people stared hard at these non-regulars without blankets or gas masks, who might want the use of theirs.

The shelter marshal could have had a German swastika on his arm band. 'What you doin' in 'ere?'

'Lost our mum. Thought she come in 'ere.'

'Name of?'

'Joyce.'

'Joyce who?'

'Joyce no one – Biddy Joyce.'

He shook his head. 'Got your identity card?'

'She's got it.'

The man gave a look to his regulars. 'Squeeze yourself in till there's a lull.' But it was mean as mutton mince. You were either one of them or you weren't; two streets made a difference. And if he and Shirley *had* been gypsies, they'd have soon been turfed out under the bombs.

But they were in. Johnnie lost Shirley's wet knickers behind the curtain where the bucket was – she could do without drawers for half a day – and settled them in to sit tight till the proper all-clear went, never mind any let up in the bombing. After which, it was going to be over Tower Bridge and a tram to Woolwich. From where it was only a step along to Plumstead nick. He knew it like the back end of Wally Stubbs's horse.

But only *her* going into the nick, thanks. Not him. Pricey would've marked his card all right, sure as eggs. But he could get Shirley as far as the door. That was a promise. He'd kept hold of her on the bus; and he could have left her to the policeman just now at the house. So there was no chance he wasn't going to see she got back to her mum. He owed her that; like any dad keeping his word.

It was all different for him, though.

Another bomb fell somewhere close and shook the shelter; the lights went out and came on again, swinging. Sand from the sandbags got in their faces, and a rumble came up through the floor like the devil showing off. An old lady started crying, and most of the rest just sat up staring. No one got up to give a song, or start 'Knees up, Mother Brown'; and if anyone had spoons it was because they were like family jewellery, not for playing percussion up and down their arms.

Outside, the shells went up from a couple of guns. Inside, they sat staring into their little dreams. *Blue birds over the white cliffs of Dover* – all that. But not him, not Johnnie Stubbs. Because his little dream had gone up the chimney with the receipt books, and his dad out of reach on a troopship, or over France, or in a prison camp, or somewhere else where no letters got through. But Pricey had done more harm than that. He'd put Johnnie Stubbs's name up in lights. And after him hanging out at Old Nell's, the police over Plumstead would be well on the look-out. They'd be all over the scrapyard like flies on a turd, with his name written up big on the police Charge Room blackboard.

And wouldn't 'Captain' Rosewarn at *HMS Greengates* start rubbing his hands when Johnnie was dragged back in by the ear . . .?

More bombs fell, and the anti aircraft guns went on trying to answer back. The lights came and went, and some old fellow croaked a prayer over and over till he was told to stuff it. In the moan of it all, Johnnie nursed himself where he ached – his head and down below; one arm for Shirley, one hand for himself.

But he was still thinking on. When the all-clear went next morning, he'd have to put his best foot forward, point his girl the right way to walk into the nick – and then vanish off the face of things like he'd never been there. There wasn't any other choice.

He looked down at the kid. She still wasn't asleep, but leaning into him and looking round the shelter, staring at those faces staring back. It was like she'd been his little kid all his life. Sort of joined together. He winked at her, and she winked back, two eyes. He reckoned if he told her to walk off the end of Southend Pier, she'd do it. And when someone trusts you like that, you owe them everything. No doubt.

He nodded at her to worm in where a drunk had turned over and left his backside hanging out of his blanket. And between the space of one bomb and the next Johnnie was in next to her. 'Not long. Stay 'ere till morning, then get you back 'ome to your mum.' And good as gold, she cuddled off to sleep, one hand holding his, the other clutching her 'Pip, Squeak and Wilfred'. And for Johnnie it made his heart go light, like bubbles in his blood. And that moment, as another bomb fell and with everything gone wrong, he knew that however he ended up, he'd never forget how good it was right now.

In the Blue Watch sleeping quarters Reg Lewis was packing his stuff. The room was empty, the rest of his watch were on their rest day, and they'd shaken his hand fit to come off, and left him to it.

He put his kit by the door ready to pick up, and went out of the temporary fire station in the school and up to where his house had been. All his walks in his stand-down time took him past it. But today would be the last for ever, before they went to Cardiff.

It looked less of a bomb scene now, more a bomb-site. Any dangerous bricks had been pulled down and stacked, and there was no need for a keep-out cordon any more. The kids could play cowboys and Indians all over it, make camps where they wanted. Not at all the place where he'd lived any more. And he had a bit of trouble finding where the Anderson shelter had been – had to line himself up with that lamppost on the pavement again. He walked on to the site, eyes on the ground like a shrapnel collector. He stopped and looked around to check that no one was staring, and when he was sure, he knelt down on the rubble, and closed his eyes, and wet the dust with the shake of his tears. He took a rosebud out of his buttonhole and he bent to the bruised earth, and kissed it, and laid the flower there.

He stood up, sniffling; drew a great breath. Out of habit he patted his pocket where his pipe was – and suddenly stooped to pick up a flake of house brick and put it in his tobacco pouch; feeling his way, because he couldn't see out of his eyes.

The hospital Sister thought he was doing wrong. As plain as Plumstead Marshes she'd said it – moving Vera was going to do for her: it'd be the thing that would finish her off. Deep down in her coma she'd know her daughter had been given up for lost. And rather than leave her behind, she'd go off 'looking for her in heaven'.

Reg didn't know what was right any more. What he'd done, he'd only done for the best. And it might be wrong, but he was posted to Cardiff now; it was all fixed. There was no about-face on that, and certainly not on the feelings in a Sister's bones.

He looked up at the clear sky, where they were bringing down the barrage balloons for repairs. He saw their silver bodies catching the sun, watched their slow ducking dance as they were wound in on their cables. Shirley was always saying she liked the sky; so he stared on up at it, past the balloons to the high cloud, and wondered where heaven was.

Riding a number 70 tram to the Woolwich Ferry was

more like being in an obstacle race. Buses could steer round the rubble; but trams could only go where the tramlines went. And when the lines went up in the air, the tram had to stop and you all had to change to another on the other side. When it came. It happened to Johnnie's trams twice: in the Old Kent Road and again at New Cross, where the overhead power wires were down.

It had been another bad night for London. From the smoke still black in the sky, you could see what a pasting the docks had taken. The air stank of fire and cordite and it tasted of brick and sour soil. Up side streets crews were still working: digging, listening, looking up at houses with the fronts off. Fireplaces in walls fifteen feet up. Everything inside out. And the raid wasn't properly over yet: no all-clear had gone, but people had come out of the shelters, business as usual. You only got paid for going to work.

Shirley liked the trams. Johnnie sat her downstairs on the first one, but she took him upstairs on the next, up at the front where it swayed and dipped like a plank in the sea. And going up the stairs or down the aisle, it was always one hand for Johnnie, and the other for her 'Pip, Squeak and Wilfred'.

The last tram conductor was a misery-guts. But being the last, Johnnie still had to ask him a favour.

'Can I 'ave a lend of your pencil, mate? 'Alf a tick?'

The man looked at Johnnie as if he'd asked for his precious ration book. 'What the devil for? Homework?'

'Put 'er name in 'er book . . .'

'Whatever next!' But he gave it to Johnnie. 'Well,

don't break the point on it.'

'Ta, mate.'

The conductor was called downstairs to punch his bell, and gently, Johnnie lifted the annual.

'Read you a story in a bit.'

First off, he had to make things easy for whatever old copper was on the desk at Plumstead. And for her.

'Now then.' There was the usual little box inside the front cover. *This book belongs to . . .* and a couple of lines for the name to sit on. He waved the pencil like a little wand round and round over the page, the way his dad did when he was going to write down something special. Sort of practice. He looked out of the window and waited for a tram stop to come up.

'Shir-ley Lew-is. That right?'

'Shirley-May-Lewis.' Shirley looked at the page, serious and proud.

'Shirley May . . .' He'd had an Auntie May. She'd owed his dad for a cooker and gone off with the milkman. Shirley watched the pencil point as the shapes made her name; and she looked up at Johnnie. 'Do the moon,' she told him.

'No, you don't draw in here. It's special.'

'Special,' Shirley repeated, wisely.

'What road?' The pencil was there, ready. But she still didn't know what road she lived in. 'Gonna see your mum, aren't you?'

'My mum.'

Shirley took back the annual and gave it a quick cuddle: opened it at a page where Pip, Squeak and Wilfred were in a funny-face contest. 'Johnnie do.'

And he started on it, pulled the faces and got her giggling. But the others on the tram weren't in the mood for silly mucking about. He found a quiet page and started on that. And in went her thumb, and round the back of his neck came that other hand, twiddling at his hair. He snuggled in, closer than ever. Because this would be the last time. And he nearly broke the conductor's pencil.

The tram finished at Woolwich. They got off and Johnnie walked the girl on towards Plumstead, and the police station. But it couldn't be fast – and nowhere near as easy as walking her in the country. Woolwich had taken a packet as bad as anywhere. Paving stones up, roads covered in rubble, a burst main ran into the Arsenal main gates like a river. It was climb up, scramble over, get round; hard on the feet – but harder still on Johnnie's heart. And he couldn't have put his hand on it to say he wasn't going a bit slow on purpose; not with every step being one step nearer to the nick, and him handing over his Shirley.

His eyes were prickly and sore, and he had a lump in his throat like a big sweet, couldn't get it down.

He squeezed her hand and she looked up at him, still clinging on to that old book. She really was a good 'un, champeen – and he was pleased he was doing the business, putting her back to rights. But there'd be no more 'Pip, Squeak and Wilfred' for him. The nick was round the next turning – and he'd probably never see Shirley May Lewis again.

All blown out of his mind with the sudden roar. A

Dornier? Anyhow, a German *something* by the lumpy running of its engine.

He looked up at the sky. You had to stop and look. The siren started up with a warning, but people came out of shops and houses, staring up at this great droning and whining, a score of planes in the sky, coming in off the river, flying up and down and round and over like wasps going mad at rotten fruit. Off the marshes and dodging and ducking, Dorniers and Heinkels, their tails being chased by a scramble of RAF Hurricanes.

Johnnie had never seen anything like it: couldn't credit how they didn't just crash into each other, all those planes so close. And he could hear their machine-guns going. He'd never seen a dogfight before. His dad had always had him in and down the shelter sharp if a Messerschmitt came close enough over Aldgate for him to see it.

But now he watched, stood and watched, gripping Shirley's hand. And it was like *Movietone News* all that way up in the sky, like on a great screen. They screamed after each other, and dived, and climbed again, round and over and up and down – till the battle took itself further down the river, away from the docks and the Arsenal, like the RAF boys were seeing the Germans off.

It made him proud to stand and watch. Proud of his dad marching off to war. He looked down at Shirley, to say something proud and brave. And he felt bad, because he hadn't noticed till then how she was shaking, going like a little leaf.

'Sorry, sweetheart! Nasty ol' noise!' Which helped him do what had to be done. 'Come on, mate!'

He held even tighter on to her hand and ran her in under the side of a wall, skirted her along as best he could, down the High Street until they came to a shop doorway just short of the police station, where the sandbags went up the wall. And the noise of the dogfight had gone.

'That's them gone!' he said. 'Gone 'ome for tea.'

He tucked himself in the doorway and looked hard down the street at the gap in the sandbags. The way into the nick. There was no one about outside – he was on the look-out for that like his life was on it. All clear. If a copper had had his head out to watch the air show, he'd gone back in now.

'Come on, mate, let's get you –' He ran Shirley as he talked, out of the doorway and up to the entrance.

But no further.

Coming in low out of nowhere was one of the Dorniers, chased by a Hurricane right over the roofs: peeled off out of the pack to be chased by its hunter. In a screaming turn it banked, seemed to go up Lakedale Road, disappearing up on Plumstead Common.

'Get in there!' Johnnie shouted. 'Good girl! Keep your 'ead down! An' give em your book. Tell 'em your name!' He let go of her grip, backed off. 'Go on!'

She didn't want it, but it was best like this. Not standing there all soppy and kissing her goodbye. When his dad had gone marching off they'd done it on the quick, which always had to be best for the parting of the ways.

'Go on, sweetheart, in you go. Back to your mum. Ol' "Pip, Squeak an' Wilfred" – you show 'em your book, and you tell 'em: "Shirley May Lewis".'

He gave her a little push in the back: gentle, ever so gentle.

'Right? Go on, then. Ta-ta.'

But he couldn't give it long bending here. A count of ten and he'd have some brave Old Bill out to see where that last German plane had gone – and that'd be Johnnie's number up. *HMS Greengates*, here I come.

'Go on, darlin'.'

But Shirley wasn't going. She was clutching round his legs like he was the last bollard on the edge of St Katharine's Docks.

'You gotta go, sweetheart! Find your mummy, eh?' And he pulled her off him, and as she failed at a grab, he ran back along the pavement to his shop doorway. She stood there, looking lost, like the orphan of all the world.

'Go on! Johnnie's gotta go! Gotta get on the road again!'

Which was when the Dornier screamed back along the curve of Plumstead High Street; well in the Hurricane's sights. Johnnie could see the glint of the cockpit shield as it roared past.

And there was Shirley still standing fixed, sobbing at him in the terrifying noise, shaking her head, reaching out.

'Shirley don't like the sky! Don't like the sky

today!'

And at the pitiful sight of her frozen there, Johnnie knew what he had to do.

Reg Lewis had heard the Dornier, was in the fire station shelter while the Hurricane chased it up the river, came out with the others when the all-clear went.

For the last time ever he crossed the playground of his old school. He deliberately didn't look at the sheds where he'd first kissed a girl, or at the chained metal drinking cup where you caught the dirty boys' germs, or at the wicket on a wall where he'd once bowled out Mr Davies. All he was about was picking up his kit and getting to the hospital. This old life was behind him, for good and all. They'd have got Vera ready to be moved, for better or worse.

But as he got to the top of the steps into the school building, Station Officer Caesar was standing in the way, and out of those walking in, Reg somehow knew he was waiting for him.

The man's face was straight, but also fighting back tears; and Bill Caesar wasn't a man who took to tears easy.

'Reg,' he said. 'A word.'

And the rest of the brigade disappeared like fireflies in daylight. It was going to be Vera. And it was going to be the worst – they'd got her ready for the move and he'd lost her already. Sister had been right.

'You aren't going to believe this; and please God –'
The man couldn't even get it out.

'Yes . . .? What? *What*, Bill?'

216

'Your girl. Shirley May Lewis?'

'Yes?' Her middle name: even her middle name . . . And Bill Caesar couldn't bring himself to say what he had to.

'Reg, as God's my judge, she's just been walked in through the door of Plumstead police station. On her two little feet. Dirty as a gypsy but as right as rain. All in one piece, by some boy . . .'

'*Shirley?*' He felt cold, his legs were going to go. It couldn't be true.

'The boy showed 'em some book, with her name in it.'

And Reg went, fell forward, and had to be caught.

In the white-tiled cell Johnnie chewed at some breakfast, but there was no chance he was going to get it down. Somewhere down the corridor he could hear Shirley crying, then shutting up, then crying again, while different coppers came and went, uncles all over the place. He wanted to get there and put his arm round her; but though they hadn't locked the door on account of his age, she could have been a million miles away. Johnnie Stubbs was out of it now. They'd all given him the big handshake, but he could tell that none of them trusted him. The girl's father was coming in, and they wanted Johnnie's story out in full. Then it was going to be back to *HMS Greengates* – which right now was sending people to collect him, a master and a male attendant with rail warrants. And a cane, sure as eggs.

That big sweet was back, stuck hard in his throat.

But although he couldn't swallow, he could damn well think. Like his dad always said, it was no good standing about like a lighthouse. You got on, you had to jump, you had to have things sorted.

A policeman looked round the door. Johnnie smiled. The policeman went away. Always smile at 'em, his dad said; it makes you look Simple Simon – an' you're not. Gives you the edge.

And, working it out – Pricey wouldn't have sung about where the old bus and Dukesey Joyce were. It was none of their business. So neither would Johnnie.

He heard Shirley scream, but like at a party. He could see the look on her face. A face he'd never see again, but one he'd never forget.

Her real dad had come.

It wasn't often Johnnie wanted to cry. And he only saved himself by fixing his mind on the one thing there was to hang on to.

He'd got away from *HMS Greengates* once, and he'd do it again, when half a chance came his way. Or, more likely, he'd *make* his own chance – because wasn't his name Johnnie Stubbs?

And he knew where the gypsy site was, no problem. So he'd go back to find Biddy, and hang out there with them till his dad came marching home.

And if his dad was one of those who never made it, then he'd stay on, if he wanted. The free life. And have his own wagon, and jump the broomstick with Biddy. Golden Syrup. And they'd have kids, one called Shirley May, and three good travelling dogs, called Pip and Squeak and Wilfred.

Bernard Ashley is a former head teacher, who is now writing full-time – he lives in South London where he was born.

Bernard's impressive list of titles suggests 35 years of realistic fiction – from picture books right up to teenage novels. Several of Bernard's books have been successfully televised and he has frequently appeared on prize lists, most recently with *Little Soldier*, which was short-listed for The Guardian Prize in 2000. In addition to his other activities Bernard Ashley also advises internationally on matters concerned with literacy. He is also a very popular visitor to schools.